RYOHGO NARITA
ILLUSTRATION BY
SUZUHITO YASUDA

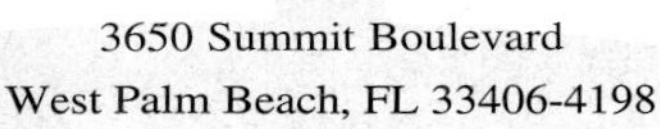

LoftBank
17:26
PHOTO ALBUM
CAMERA ROLL
罪歌
SAIKA
黄巾賊
YELLOW SCARVES
DOLLARS
な-9-

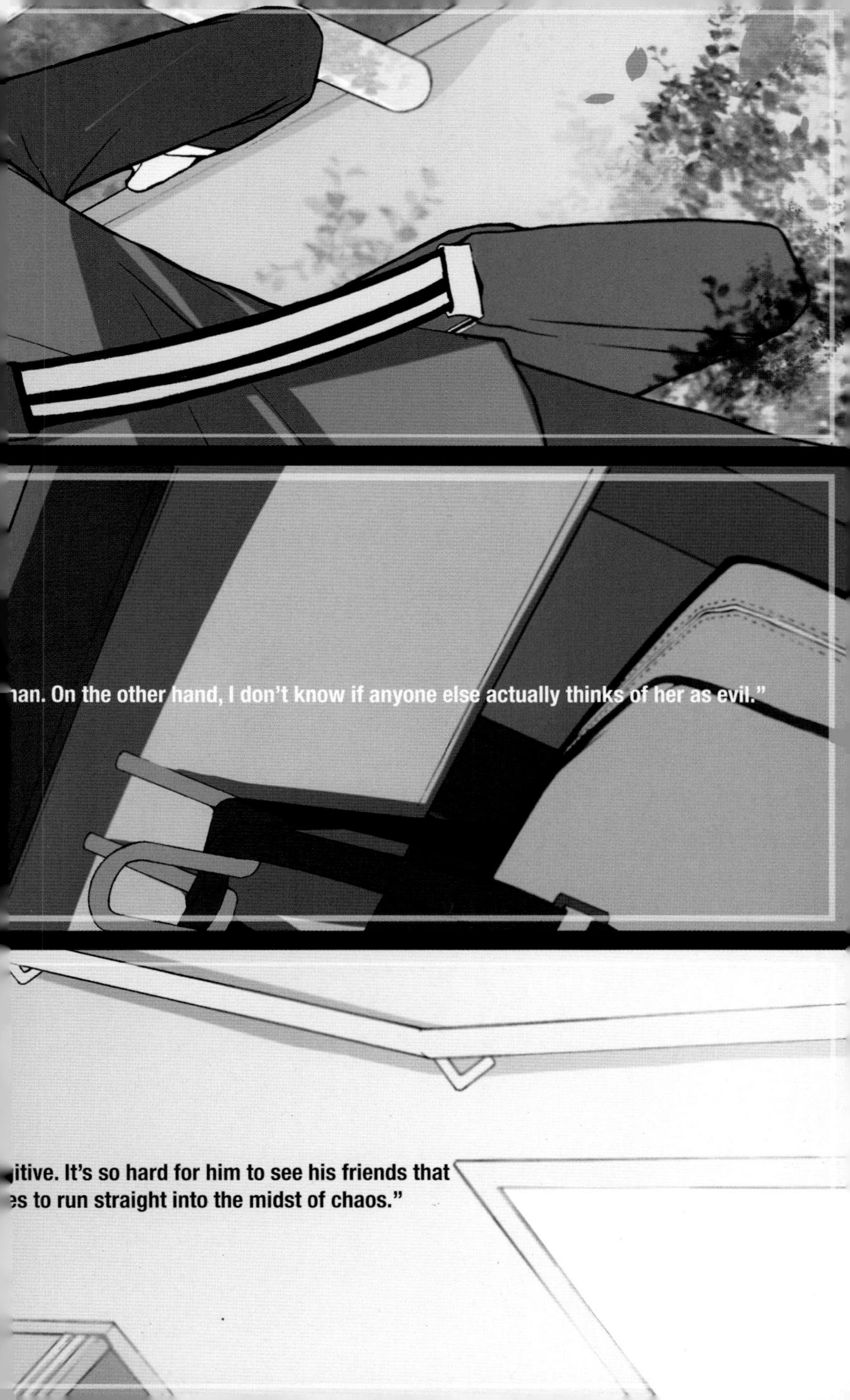
nan. On the other hand, I don't know if anyone else actually thinks of her as evil."
itive. It's so hard for him to see his friends that
es to run straight into the midst of chaos."

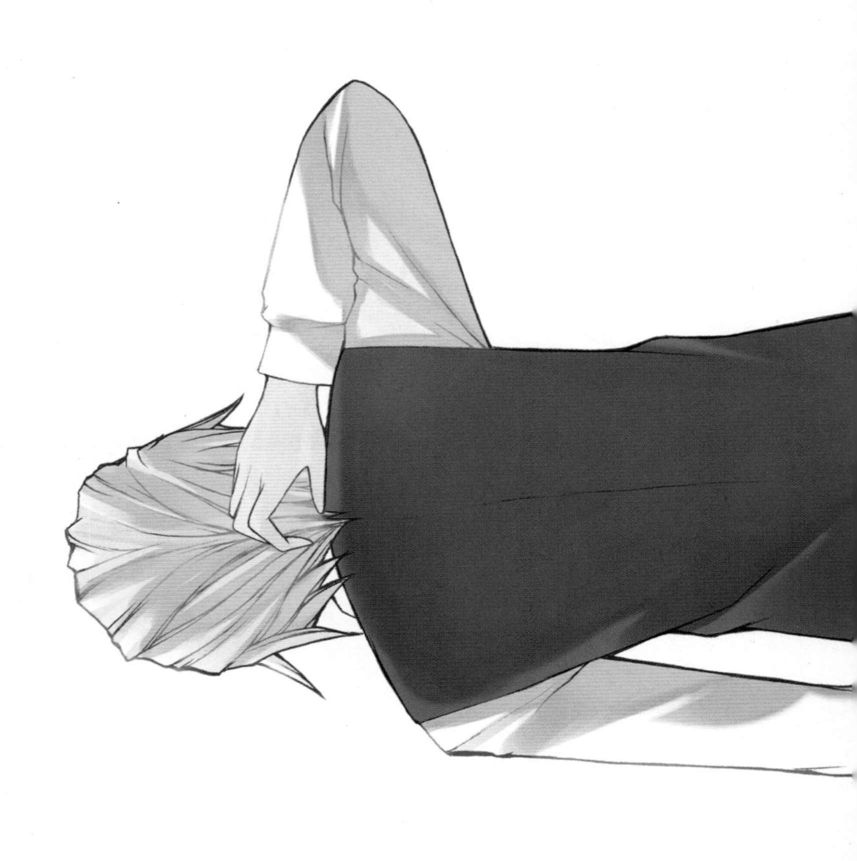

VOLUME 5

Ryohgo Narita
ILLUSTRATION BY Suzuhito Yasuda

New York

DURARARA!!, Volume 5
RYOHGO NARITA
ILLUSTRATION BY SUZUHITO YASUDA

Translation by Stephen Paul
Cover art by Suzuhito Yasuda

Edited by ASCII MEDIA WORKS
First published in 2009 by KADOKAWA CORPORATION, Tokyo.
English translation rights arranged with KADOKAWA CORPORATION, Tokyo, through Tuttle-Mori Agency, Inc., Tokyo.

Yen On
1290 Avenue of the Americas
New York, NY 10104

Visit us at yenpress.com
facebook.com/yenpress
twitter.com/yenpress
yenpress.tumblr.com
instagram.com/yenpress

First Yen On Edition: November 2016

Yen On is an imprint of Yen Press, LLC.
The Yen On name and logo are trademarks of Yen Press, LLC.

Library of Congress Cataloging-in-Publication Data
Names: Narita, Ryōgo, 1980– author. | Yasuda, Suzuhito, illustrator. | Paul, Stephen (Translator), translator.
Title: Durarara!! / Ryohgo Narita, Suzuhito Yasuda, translation by Stephen Paul.
Description: New York, NY : Yen ON, 2015–
Identifiers: LCCN 2015041320| ISBN 9780316304740 (v. 1 : pbk.) | ISBN 0316304743 (v. 1 : pbk.) | ISBN 9780316304764 (v. 2 : pbk.) | ISBN 031630476X (v. 2 : pbk.) | ISBN 9780316304771 (v. 3 : pbk.) | ISBN 0316304778 (v. 3 : pbk.) | ISBN 9780316304788 (v. 4 : pbk.) | ISBN 0316304786 (v. 4 : pbk.) | ISBN 9780316304795 (v. 5 : pbk.) | ISBN 0316304794 (v. 5 : pbk.)
Subjects: | CYAC: Tokyo (Japan)—Fiction. | BISAC: FICTION / Science Fiction / Adventure.
Classification: LCC PZ7.1.N37 Du 2015 | DDC [Fic]—dc23
LC record available at http://lccn.loc.gov/2015041320

ISBNs: 978-0-316-30479-5 (paperback)
978-0-316-30496-2 (ebook)

10 9 8 7 6 5 4 3 2 1

LSC-C

Printed in the United States of America

Let's play a game.

Don't worry. It's a very simple wager.

As easy as whether a coin lands heads or tails.

That's how straightforward it is.

Your odds are basically even; you just have to guess which of the two it will be.

For example, let's say you punch the first person to walk past this apartment building.

We'd be betting on whether the person gets angry and fights back or whether they run off crying instead.

See? A simple bet, right?

In this game, the piece you're playing with is the human mind.

Anticipating the actions and emotions of a human being.

...

Oh, come on, don't just clam up on me.

Let's say I ask you this question: "Can every person be bought or not?"

The crux of the question is the word *every*.

The answer is "Sometimes they can and sometimes they can't," right?

Sometimes people would choose their pride and conscience over ten billion yen, and sometimes they would kill for a single yen. Isn't that right? Even the same person can be wildly different, depending on the time and place.

See, the people who lose the game of life are generally the ones who decide on an answer to that question. Those who continue choosing the same answer with firm belief are one thing, but the people who unthinkingly answer either "You can't buy love" or "Even love can be bought with money" are the ones who lose the game because they can't see any other possibility. Belief in a single answer illuminates what is in front of you, but it also narrows your view. Those are simple pros and cons, wouldn't you say?

In that sense, the human mind becomes more of a bet, doesn't it?

Naturally, knowing or not knowing the target beforehand will influence your decision, but that's no different from having information about the horses in a race before it starts.

You might be affronted and claim that the human mind doesn't have the same odds as a coin flip—but the results might as well be the same thing. The only way to know for sure is if you understand the contents of the person's mind perfectly, and no one can fully fathom a mind that isn't their own.

Let's say the bet is that a certain person will commit murder or not.

The people who would say "I can't believe they'd do such a thing" in an interview are the ones who guessed heads before the flip—they thought the odds were higher that this person would never take a life. Let's assume they're not just putting on a good face for the TV camera. This is only an example, after all.

You see, the problem is, you just don't know until you open the lid.

It's impossible to completely manipulate another person.

I've done a lot of that sort of thing for fun as an information broker, but I can't control a person's mind to 100 percent certainty.

All I do is give them a push.

Not into the road when the light is red. I mean it in a different way.

When someone is treading an extremely dangerous boundary and might step on either side, I just...*push*. To make sure they take that next big step in life without hesitation.

I'm kind of a philanthropist, really.

But it's not a business, so I make no guarantees about what happens after that.

So with that in mind...let's begin the game.

Now, when I play, I give my piece a little push on the back. Just to make sure I get the result I want.

You might be able to protect the piece's back. What do you say?

Don't make that face at me.

It's like you're saying I'm incorrigible, unrepentant scum.

Games are meant to be enjoyed.

Isn't that right?

The Black Market Doctor Gets Sappy, Part One

Am I a bad guy?

Well, obviously.

I think that lying to you is the worst thing I could do, but as I said before, I don't regret it at all.

What's wrong? Why is your neck getting red?

I'm just kidding, Celty. I mean, you don't even have blood to— Ow, ow, ow, that hurts, sorry, I'm sorry.

Anyway, every time I say that I love you, you always have the same response.

"You must have been a very lonely youth."

And that's very mean of you. I wasn't lonely at all. Because I had you, of course.

What's that? You wish I would use the same first-person pronoun in Japanese rather than mixing them all together?

Oh, Celty. Don't you know the saying "Spend three years scrubbing a soapberry, and it will still be black"? It means that you can't just ask me to change my nature and expect a sudden change. The different first-person pronouns are *meant* to be switched between depending on the person you're talking to, of course.

Since the world is full of different people, I have to change my pronouns constantly…but to me, *you* are all of humanity, my entire world. That's right—I always show you each and every side of myself, including the ones I show others as well as the ones I save just for you!

…Um, what were we talking about again?

Oh, right. About evil people. Why would you bring that up out of the blue?

Aha, the movie you watched. Yes, the kind of story where all the characters are essentially good and yet they all end up committing evil deeds due to circumstances out of their control.

That's so cute that you came to ask me if I'm evil because a movie moved you.

I love that direct, honest side of you. I hope you watch a dreamy romantic movie next and say that you wish you could have a torrid romance like that.

…"Only if it's *The War of the Roses*?" You know…sometimes you can be very cruel, Celty.

Let's get back to the discussion of evil.

If it's for the sake of my love for you, no matter how horrific, I'm confident that I can be as evil as necessary.

Don't use love as an excuse? C'mon, don't be like that. The emotion of love is completely unrelated to good and evil.

Anyway, you often hear the phrase *such and such of love and good*, but you never hear about the *such and such of love and evil*.

The villain with love deeper than the ocean.

How many of those people exist, do you suppose?

If you narrowed the target down to you, I suppose it would be me.

Don't be embarrassing?

But around you, Celty, embarrassment and kinkshaming are my bread and butter.

"Stop it, I'm the one being embarrassed"? It's fine! There's another saying that goes "The fallen petal rides the flowing current." It means that if you are embarrassed, I'll hold your bashful body and *vwuh!*

Hey, you didn't have to hit me. Seems more like this flowing current doesn't want to carry the flower petal!

Still, I like that contrarian side of your personality, Celty; it's very cu— Owwww! Aha, you're pinching my cheek to hide your shy-ai-ai-ai-aiiiie! You're gonna pull my sheek offfh! Youw gowwa puwwa weew waww!

Chapter 1
DRRR!! DRR5
NA9-30
Ryohgo Narita
THE FIGHTING PUPPET SUBTLY FRETS

May 3, Sunshine, Sixtieth Floor Street, Ikebukuro

Sunshine 60 Street, one of the most famous in Ikebukuro.

Commonly called "Sixtieth Floor Street," it heads from the east exit of the train station toward the Sunshine building, a stretch of shops that is one of the biggest destinations for visitors coming to Ikebukuro by train.

It's a shortcut from the station to the Sunshine building and is occasionally lumped in with the adjacent Sunshine Street, but they are in fact separate roads.

The time is Golden Week, the cluster of holidays within a week of each other in the spring.

Given the start of the long holiday, the foot traffic on the street was more bustling than usual.

Families on their way to Sunshine City, couples headed for one of the countless movie theaters in the area, youngsters seeking new clothes, hungry salarymen, Akiba nerds heading to specialty shops like Toranoana and Manga no Mori, women on their way to Animate or the butler café Swallowtail—people with varying destinations crossed paths on the sidewalks, where they were set upon by barkers of similarly varying stripes: handsome men from host clubs, women hawking art, even towering foreigners.

Along this street, right as you enter from Ikebukuro Station, there is one spot that draws the attention: the Cinema Sunshine building with its massive street-facing monitor and gaudy movie posters.

The video arcade on the first floor has numerous entertainment machines on display, most notably a line of "UFO catcher" crane games at the entrance, where youngsters like to hang out and kill time before their movie starts.

"Hey, Rocchi! Get that one next! That one, the plushie!"

"Aww, no fair! He already got one for you, Non!"

At the entrance to the arcade, a group of girls was congregated around a UFO catcher, their squeals of delight setting the peaceful and lively scene.

"Hey, Rocchi, I wanna try it, too."

"Oh, then while Kanacchi's playing it, let's go and buy some drinks, Rocchi."

"Wait a second, you're just going to leave me here all alone?"

"Yeah, why not? You've got a Yukichi today, Kanacchi. Why don'cha cash it out and do your alien thing surrounded by Hideyos? Ew, I just brain scanned that image! What a freak factory. Total GB."

"...Um, Kiyomin, what did she just say?"

"If you want it translated into Japanese, she said, 'Kana, you brought a ten-thousand-yen bill today, so just change it for smaller bills and play the UFO catcher and get left out by the rest of the group. I just imagined it. It was a very weird picture to imagine. I got goose bumps.' ...Or something along those lines. Creepy. I wish she'd just speak in Japanese."

"Eww, Kiyosuke, don't translate it all weird like that. It's such a buzzkill. And, like, if anyone's being an alien, it's you."

With that rather typical conversation, the group of ten or so left the arcade behind—but then the ordinary scene was pierced by an unordinary sound.

"Move it, damn you!" snorted an agitated man among the paradise of pedestrians.

The crowds automatically turned to look in the direction of the disturbance and saw a middle-aged man wearing a hat, trying to race down the street and pushing aside anyone standing in his way.

The crowds weren't as dense as a station platform during rush hour, so with a bit of well-considered coordination, he could have darted and slipped his way through cleanly, but he was so agitated that it was essentially a straight beeline down the concrete.

Far behind him, a woman was in pursuit, limping and shouting something after him. What she was yelling was unclear, but she appeared to be wearing a retail uniform. Based on the desperate look on her face, it seemed likely that the man had committed a robbery or had shoplifted.

The people milling around were paralyzed with confusion in the moment, but as understanding sank in, a few tried to block the man's path.

"Outta the damn way!" he slurred, frantic and out of breath. He bowled his blockers over; up close, he was not tall, but quite muscular, and charged through anyone in his way like a football linebacker.

"Whoa, crap! Look out!" "Where's Shizuo and Simon when you need them?"

"Let's get outta here!" "Call the cops!" "He's coming this way!"

"Hey, snap a pic!" "Come on, have some respect!"

"No, I mean to get a shot of his face for evidence!" "Oh, right."

"Yikes, it's too late!" "Who is that, Daddy?" "Stay close to me."

"Что случилось?" *(What happened?)*

"Нет проблем." *(No problem.)*

"Huh?! What's this, Kuru?! What's going on?!"

"Silence."

"I didn't notice because I was busy reading a dirty mag. What's the commotion?"

"Quiet."

Wildly different voices collided and intersected, creating an instantaneous buzz throughout the street—the perfect stage for another abnormal figure to appear.

The group of girls just leaving the arcade pulled backward so as not to get stuck in the uproar, and a single man emerged as he strode forward.

At first glance, he seemed like any other young man. He wore a number of thin, light layers, like a fashion model who sprang right out of the pages of a magazine. His style was more mature and less wild, more fitting of the Daikanyama or Omotesando neighborhoods than Ikebukuro—but what set him apart was his face.

It was not particularly notable for its beauty or lack thereof. If anything, it was hard to tell which of the two his visage would be considered.

In the shade of the straw hat, bandages covered his forehead, their surface blotted with red blood. There was a medical eyepatch covering one eye, the kind used to cover up a sty, and a large Band-Aid on his cheek. A dark bruise extended from the edge of the bandage. He looked like he'd either been hit by a bat or tumbled down the stairs and smacked his face on the ground.

"Umm, Rocchi? Watch out, you're already hurt," one of the girls started to stay, but the man named Rocchi was already walking straight into the escape path of the barging tackler.

"I told you, get the f—" the muscular man bellowed, lowering himself and speeding up to overpower the youth.

But the injured young man only lifted up a foot to kick at his assailant.

The move was a "yakuza kick" in pro wrestling parlance, in which the bottom of the attacking foot is planted firmly on the target. There was once an old-school giant wrestler who called it the Size 16 Kick, a flashy attack that knocked the target backward.

If the kicker's foot made contact with the charging man's shoulder, it should have thrown him off-balance and tossed him backward. In fact, everyone present assumed that the young man on one leg was going to be hurled off his feet.

But they were wrong.

An ugly scraping sound rent the air.

The source of the sound was evident after considering the young man's new position several feet back, still in the same pose—and a black line extending from the tip of his grounded foot.

The young man had stopped the muscular man's charge with the bottom of his raised foot and merely slid back a short distance. The shift in momentum that had occurred within his body must have been tremendous.

The instantaneous, phenomenal transfer of force left a line of black, charred shoe sole on the asphalt. The trail was practically smoking.

And the tackling man did not attempt to take another step.

If he'd planted one more step at his original speed, he could have tossed the youngster aside, as everyone imagined. But right at that last step, the point at which he'd have put the most power into his charge, he couldn't.

The young man's kick had thrown his heel directly into the mouth of the charging man, flattening it into his face.

"You just knocked over three women?" the young man growled coldly, but the man could hardly have heard the words.

"Grgh…guh."

His front teeth were no doubt broken already. He could only groan in uncomprehending pain, the heel of the shoe jammed into his mouth.

The young man's good eye narrowed.

"Three times."

He swiveled his toes left and right thrice, all his weight pressing on the man's face. He was stepping on the man, trampling him as he stood.

With fine little cracking sounds, the man's nose *turned* like the knob on a gas stove.

"Aaaa— Aaa— Aaa— Aaaah! Aaah! Aaah!"

The fresh wave of pain must have brought him to his senses. The man screamed and wailed helplessly, covering his gushing nose and rolling on the pavement.

The young man looked down at him as if he were a mosquito felled by bug spray.

Meanwhile, the group of girls looking on from a safe distance did not seem particularly shocked or surprised.

"Why's Rocchi so fired up?"

"Didn't you see the employee chasing after that guy was a woman?"

"Another woman. It never ends with him."

"Well, what are you gonna do? Rocchi's a womanizer."

"It's part of what makes him so charming."

"Exactly."

* * *

But Rocchi was more focused on the female employee approaching him than the conversation of the girls behind him.

"Th-thank you… He was shoplifting from our store," the uniformed employee panted. Her voice was trembling, either from the exertion of running so long and hard or from fear of the young man standing over his bloodied victim.

The young man doffed his hat and gently took her hand, murmuring, "Not at all. I only did what anyone would do."

His voice was so soft and sweet, it was almost silly. The facial features peeking out from behind the eyepatch and bandages softened into a smile, and he was suddenly an entirely different person from the one who had just kicked a grown man to the curb.

The suddenly benign young man glanced down at the woman's leg with concern.

"Why, miss. Your leg is scraped."

"Huh…? Oh, er…that happened when I tried to stop him, and he pushed me…"

"…"

Without removing the pleasant smile from his face, the young man spun around on his heel—and leaped.

"?"

The woman flinched, momentarily bewildered by his action.

But she understood what he was doing right after.

Right at the point where his feet landed was the attempted shoplifter's leg, still lying on the ground. He landed directly on the man's knee with all his weight.

The ugly crunching sound was only briefly audible before the man's scream drowned it out.

"Dabaaah! Ah! Dah! Aaaga-ga-ga-ga-a-ga-da-da-da-dah!"

"Shut your mouth, scumbag," the young man commanded in a chilling tone. He kicked the man hard in the crotch.

"————!!!"

"I'm assuming that even *you* have a wife, or a daughter, or a mother, so for their sakes, I'm not gonna kill you right here and now. But what kind of man attacks a woman at all? Am I right?"

"——! ——————!!"

The shoplifter twitched in agony on the ground, all the air expelled from his lungs.

All the helpless onlookers crowding around the scene felt time stop around them, but the young man merely returned to his gentle smile and remarked, "Don't worry. Everything's all right. I've taken the liberty of enacting your revenge for you."

"..."

The woman was still stunned into silence. He continued casually, "Vengeance doesn't suit a beautiful lady like you. For real. Er, seriously. Just let me handle all the dirty work—"

He was interrupted by a different woman's voice.

"Rocchi."

"Oh? What is it, Non?"

He spun around to see the shortest of the group of girls that he came with. The girl named Non tugged on Rocchi's sleeve and said frankly, "Kiyo says we ought to take off now because that was excessive self-defense."

"Oh. Really?"

He turned back to the unconscious shoplifter twitching on the ground, then glanced at the store employee.

She was blinking in silence, but there was less gratitude in her gaze than sheer terror.

"...Uh-oh, Non. I seem to have frightened her."

"I told you, we gotta run. Look, the police are coming."

"Ooh, you're right."

Across the massive intersection in the direction of the station, police uniforms could be spotted among the crowd waiting for the light to change.

"Well, pretty lady, I've got to get going. You don't want to develop a limp, so go to a doctor to get your leg checked..."

"Come on, Rocchi! Hurry up!"

"H-hey, wait... Non! When did you get to be such a selfish...? Fine, fine! I'm coming, I'm coming! Oh, and miss! If that guy wakes up, tell him something for me! I can usually be found riding highways all over Saitama, so if he's got a problem, he can find me there... *Owww!* I'm coming! Just stop pulling on my ear, Non! Nonnn!"

The young man was dragged back to the group of girls, who took off running with him in tow.

Some of the crowd left behind after the scene had tried to snap pictures with their phones, but the young man was hidden among the group in no time, so the only photo evidence they could collect was of the shoplifter, who seemed like both the criminal and the victim in this case.

♂♀

After the hubbub, the crowd was left curious about the identity of the young man.

"And here he is," muttered a man sitting inside a Lotteria fast-food joint, who had witnessed the entire exchange. "Ugh, this is gonna be a pain."

The bespectacled, dreadlocked debt collector grimaced. Another man, who was wearing a bartender's uniform for some reason, approached and said, "Got you some coffee, Tom… What's wrong?"

"Oh, thanks. Just…saw a familiar face, that's all."

Shizuo Heiwajima, the man in the bartender's outfit, sat easily across from his supervisor, Tom. Either the commotion from moments earlier hadn't drawn his notice or he didn't particularly care about it either way.

"You saw a friend?"

"No, I wouldn't call him that," murmured Tom, who sipped his black coffee. "If anything, he's probably here for you."

"?"

"Remember how you beat up that biker gang from Saitama last month? Walloped them, really."

"…Yeah. The ones who ripped my clothes…"

Tom noticed Shizuo's expression darkening and chose to tread carefully to avoid angering his partner.

"I just saw the leader of Toramaru, that very biker gang."

"…"

"His name's Chikage Rokujou. Normally, he walks around with—well, gets dragged around by—a group of girls during the day. But he's still a gang leader. He ain't the kind to set your house on fire, but you oughta watch out for him all the same."

Shizuo remained silent for a time, reflecting on Tom's words, then asked, "Is he the guy with a leather jacket and some kinda white heart mark on it?"

"Oh, you're familiar? Yeah, that's kind of like their uniform, so he only wears it at night."

"He showed up yesterday."

"Huh?" Tom gawked, holding his coffee in front of his face with an arched eyebrow.

Shizuo chewed on a mouthful of burger and described the previous night's events.

"Well...I was on my way home when this guy on a motorcycle came up."

♂♀

The previous evening, Ikebukuro

"Yo, how's it going?"

"?"

He turned around at the sudden greeting and saw a motorcycle stopped nearby, with a young man standing in front of the idle vehicle.

"You Shizuo Heiwajima? Yeah, I figured. You don't see many guys wandering around dressed like bartenders. I hear you're a pretty big deal around here."

"...?"

"I hear some members of our team got a beatdown, courtesy of you."

"Team?"

Chikage Rokujou chattered amiably, "Look, I've heard they were carryin' on where they shouldn't, so I'm takin' that into account; it's their problem. But you hospitalized 'em all. Even if it was our fault, I think I've got a right to be a bit upset here, don't you?"

The young man, half a head shorter than Shizuo, smiled cockily and leaned in until they were a breath apart.

"What do you suppose they said to me from their hospital beds? That you pulled a streetlight out of the ground and swung it around. I thought they musta taken a bad blow to the head, but today I come and see a streetlight paved into a brand-new patch of concrete."

"And...?"

"Given my position, I'm naturally feeling curious about what you can do. Oh...by the way, you got any women who would cry over you?"

"Huh?" Shizuo grunted.

Chikage shot him a toothy grin. "I'm just saying, if you did, I'd be fine with dropping this whole thing. It's not my style to make women cry."

Anyone who knew Shizuo would assume that by now he'd reach the boiling point and throw that monstrous fist of his. But instead of looking furious, he had an expression of sudden understanding.

"...Oh, I see. It makes sense now."

"What does?"

"You're picking a fight with me."

"Uh, yeah," Chikage mumbled, surprised that the conversation had taken a few steps backward.

"Gotcha, gotcha. Haven't had such a straightforward approach since high school. Speaking of, I'm a fully grown adult now, but you're just a kid, a teenager still. Even if you did beat me, you wouldn't get to brag about it at school."

"What does age have to do with a fight? Did you learn how to chat working as a bartender?"

"If only," Shizuo chuckled. He cracked his neck. "I actually kinda like it when people are so straight with me, in fact. But the best option is not coming after me at all."

"Sorry about that."

"Oh, and there's one thing I should say."

They were standing quite close to each other, but right as Shizuo was going to tell the other man something—

No sooner had Shizuo removed his glasses than his field of vision was filled with shoe soles.

With a heavy thud, both of Chikage's feet slammed into Shizuo's face.

The instant Shizuo had opened his mouth to speak, Chikage used the sidewalk fence nearby as a launching pad to throw a full-body dropkick, more of a pro wrestling move than an actual street-fight technique.

However, right as he thought, *Got him!*—Chikage realized something felt different.

Huh?

Why won't he go down?

It felt like that one time he'd leaped off an especially thick stalk of bamboo, and a terrible chill ran through his entire body.

Chikage managed to maintain his balance as he landed, and he used the full momentum to bounce off the ground and up into a fierce punch.

Even so, something was wrong.

...

...Huh?

...Did I punch the ground just now?

There was indeed a sensation of soft flesh at the end of his fist, but whatever the material was, it did not yield. His fist just stopped short, as if he were punching straight into the ground. Chills and question marks swirled within Chikage's head.

Shizuo repeated, "There's one thing I should mention... Like my name says, I just want to live in peace and quiet."

"...What?"

Chikage's eyes went wide. Yes, his fist was touching the other man's cheek.

But at best, it tilted Shizuo's face and hadn't changed the man's expression in the least. He was acting as though he hadn't even been touched.

"So I need you..."

"Wha—?!"

The skin-colored mass burst straight through the accomplished street fighter's guard.

"...t o g o t o s l e e p."

Unlike with Chikage's punch, this fist hit its target and buried itself deep into the flesh.

♂♀

"...And then you sent him to Sleepytown, like always," Tom noted, sipping his coffee. Meanwhile, Shizuo tugged at the straw of his vanilla shake.

"Yeah. Well, I took him to a doctor I know."

"Really? You took someone to the doctor?"

"Didn't want him to end up dying. Also, I didn't really hate the guy. If he was a total fleabrain, I'd have finished him off for good."

"Then again, a single punch from you is basically fatal as it is," Tom noted wryly.

But Shizuo interjected, "Four."

"Huh?"

"He kept getting up until the *fourth* punch."

"...Seriously?" Tom murmured, the sugar packet falling through his fingers.

"I think the last thing he said before I could punch him a fifth time was, 'I got a girl who will take care of me in the hospital, aren't you jealous?' But he broke a tooth, so it was kind of hard to make out—maybe I misheard. Anyway, that's when he fell over."

"...I mean, I knew he was tough, but still."

"Actually, you'd be surprised. The foreign guy who showed up a while back took several shots, too."

"Yeah, well, the world's a big place... It's also wild that he's up on his feet and walking around today. But I guess they're just facial wounds..."

"To be honest, I actually am jealous that he has a girl to take care of him."

"Right, you don't have a girlfriend. Well, when you're just hanging around eating lunch with a dude all the time, it does feel kinda empty. Would be nice to have a more *gentle* relationship to engage in, ya know? I guess even you could want something like that, yeah?" Tom asked. Maybe because of how far back they went, Tom dared to ask Shizuo a personal question. Most people familiar with Shizuo would be too scared to ask such a question, but Tom had been with him long enough to understand his boundaries and what made him angry.

Sure enough, Shizuo simply nodded and grunted in the affirmative before complaining, "The only person who's ever said she loved me might not even count as a woman."

"Huh? Why, you go to gay bars or trans pubs or something?"

"No, I'm not talking about them. I don't even know if she's human... more like a blade..."

"Okay, you've totally lost me there," Tom said, baffled.

Shizuo thought back on the days of his youth. "Girls have pretty much never wanted anything to do with me. Part of it is my own personality, but I also hung around with that fleabrain and the four-eyed freak in school. Fleabrain would trick the girls into going with him somewhere, and the crazy one was so creepy that none of them ever bothered to approach."

"You talkin' about Izaya and that…doctor guy you mentioned earlier?"

"Yeah, he was real logical and fussy, too, so I would snap on him all the time, but I guess we were just destined to sort of hang around together. But I do wish that fleabrain would just rot away and die already. At any rate, I don't seem to have much luck with human women."

"Hey, don't worry about it. You could get a girlfriend anytime you want. You look a lot like your brother, and he's a superstar," Tom ad-libbed.

Shizuo merely looked surprised and wondered, "You think we look that alike?"

Up until this point, it was just another ordinary day for them—for Shizuo Heiwajima in particular.

The incident with Chikage Rokujou should have been nothing more than a momentary spice to liven up the very mundane day.

But when it ended, it took the mundane part with it.

Abnormal, extraordinary occurrences were by their very definition rare, so when the ordinary came to an end, it was always abrupt.

But in the moment of this particular shift, neither man realized it had happened.

Because the dawn of this extraordinary occurrence to Shizuo Heiwajima appeared as anything but.

"Since we had Lotteria for lunch, maybe we should balance it out with McDonald's for dinner… Wha—?" Tom squawked abruptly.

Shizuo looked up, a question mark floating over his head.

"What's the matter?"

"Behind you."

"?"

Shizuo was sitting at a table with his back to the window that faced out on Sixtieth Floor Street. Tom directed his attention over Shizuo's shoulder toward the street.

"What's behind—?" Shizuo started to say, then closed his mouth.

Squish.

That was the best way to describe the scene before him.

A girl was on the other side of the store window. The small figure had both palms and her forehead flattened tight against the glass, staring intently at Shizuo.

"..."

For a second, Shizuo thought it was Kururi or Mairu, two girls he knew. He couldn't imagine any other girls flattening themselves against a window, staring at him, smack in the middle of Ikebukuro.

But this girl's face was different, and she was clearly too young to be Mairu or Kururi. If anything, this girl seemed to be no older than elementary school age, ten years old at best.

"...?"

The girl was staring hard at Shizuo's face. She dropped her gaze momentarily to a scrap of paper she was holding and then went back to gazing at the young man in the bartender outfit.

Her features bloomed into a flowery smile.

It wasn't a polite smile or a shy smile, but the innocent beaming of a child that just got a toy it wanted.

The girl tottered back and forth like a wind-up figurine, spinning around in front of the store as she stared at Shizuo.

"...Is that a relative of yours?"

"...Nope. Not ringing a bell."

"And that wasn't the look of someone who saw a rare outfit and wanted to gawk."

"Nope. I'll go out and see what's up," Shizuo said, getting to his feet to find the answer to this mystery.

"Wait, really? What if she starts off with 'Papa!' or 'Darling' or something?"

"This is real life, not one of Yumasaki's fantasies."

He cleared his tray and headed outside, where the girl was still watching him with sparkling eyes. Many parents liked to praise their children for having features "like a doll," but if anyone was worthy of the phrase, it was this girl.

Her shoulder-length black hair shone in the sun, and her cutely bobbed bangs bounced, covering her eyes one at a time as her head tilted left and right.

Despite the warmth of May, she had a double-breasted jacket on. It was a formal child's outfit of foreign style, and despite the gaudiness of the gold buttons, it was rather chic in appearance.

But the way her hair always covered one eye gave her a strangely gloomy appearance overall, even with the smile.

The girl stared straight at Shizuo and trotted over to him without hesitation.

Trotted closer.

Trotted closer.

Trotted, trotted

Trotted trotted trotted

trot trot trot trot trot

trot-tot-tot-tot-tot

Something feels wrong.

An unfathomable, indescribable wave of unpleasantness ran down Shizuo's back.

There's something about the way she's smiling.

If you called that "innocent," it would sound so nice.

But this one's an awful lot like those worn by kids who stomp on lines of ants...

The words that tumbled out of the girl's mouth confirmed his suspicion.

"Drop dead."

And then, the girl drove a modified stun gun straight into Shizuo's midsection.

The next instant, there was a terrific crackling sound in the air as electricity jumped—

And Shizuo Heiwajima was gently pulled into the realm of the extraordinary.

Chat room, one night earlier (May 2)

Setton has entered the chat.

Setton: Evenin'.
Setton: Oh? No one's here.
Setton: I'll just wait.
Setton: Hang on, my partner's calling me, so I'm stepping away for a moment.

TarouTanaka has entered the chat.

TarouTanaka: Good evening.
TarouTanaka: Is it just you, Setton?
TarouTanaka: Oh, no response.
TarouTanaka: I guess you're still busy with whatever it is. Sorry.
TarouTanaka: I'll just wait.

Kuru has entered the chat.
Mai has entered the chat.

Kuru: Forgive me for intruding when you are so occupied with your waiting. Tarou waits despite knowing that the other is around, and Setton has left, not realizing that there are now others to speak with anew. Is it a hint of romance I detect? Oh, but I do not know either of your genders. Perhaps the male moniker "Tarou" in fact belongs to a woman. And the name Setton
Mai: ?
Kuru: Pardon me. I hit the character limit. Anyway, the name Setton is not innately gendered. By the way, it is a very curious username to have. Where does it come from? I just did an Internet search and found it is the name of a piece of traditional Korean clothing. Is that it? Or did you borrow it from the movie producer Maxwell Setton?
Mai: It's a mystery.
Setton: I'm back. Evenin'.
Setton: Wow, very intense people.
Setton: Oh no. My username is just a play on my actual name.

Kuru: My goodness, I did not realize it was such a simple reason. Oh dear, I just called you simple. Please accept my deepest apologies and recognize that it was a harmless mistake. But do you realize that you have given us an angle to decipher your identity? What wrinkle did you use to hide your original name? You could be Sanpei Seto… Anna Setouchi… You have made yourself an even greater mystery to me.
Mai: Jiro-Saburo-Tonpei Serata.
Setton: Tonpei?
Mai: —(This message contains an inappropriate word and cannot be displayed)—
Mai: Huh?
Setton: Whoa, what function is that? I've never seen it before.
Setton: …And seriously, what did you think my username was short for?
Mai: —(This message contains an inappropriate word and cannot be displayed)—
Mai: Oh, you can't type that word.
Mai: Ouch.
Setton: ?
Mai: I got pinched.
Kuru: Please forgive me. We are using separate computers next to each other, and I noticed that Mai was entering a terribly rude word and took it upon myself to punish her in real life for soiling the mood. Please be reassured that I am in control.
Setton: You two seem to get along.

Bacura has entered the chat.

Bacura: 'Suuup.
Kuru: Oh, it's the playboy who plays the recorder.
Mai: Good evening.
Bacura: Are you still on about the recorder thing?!
Setton: Evenin'.

Saika has entered the chat.

Bacura: Ooh, just one minute off.
Setton: You're in sync.

Saika: good evening
Bacura: Did Tarou already fall asleep?
Bacura: It's only ten o'clock still,
Bacura: How much of a healthy little mama's boy is that guy?
TarouTanaka: Whoa, I was on the phone and went to the bathroom, and now everyone's here!
TarouTanaka: Good evening, everybody.
Bacura: Speak of the devil.
Setton: It's synchronicity.
Bacura: In Japanese that sounds like the last level of a video game: Shin Kuroni City!
TarouTanaka: I honestly couldn't care less.

<Private Mode> Bacura: Mikado.
<Private Mode> Bacura: We need to talk.
<Private Mode> TarouTanaka: Uh...

Setton: Kuroni City, huh?
Saika: what does it mean

<Private Mode> TarouTanaka: Masaomi...is that you?
<Private Mode> Bacura: ...That doesn't matter now, does it?
<Private Mode> TarouTanaka: Well, I've been following your lead and pretending not to recognize you for the past two months...

Kuru: One wonders what possible thought process could have produced that comment from Bacura... The human mind is truly an unfathomable thing. Perhaps the human mind is in sync with countless forms of madness. I only hope that madness does not threaten all mankind.

<Private Mode> TarouTanaka: Sorry, when I said I couldn't possibly care less, I was just joking around.
<Private Mode> TarouTanaka: Look, I don't know what to say, but I didn't expect that I'd be talking to you in open acknowledgment of your identity. I just didn't think you'd be so angry about it. Of course I care about you, Masaomi! That Shin Kuroni City joke was great and super-funny.

<Private Mode> Bacura: No, I'm not talking about that.
<Private Mode> Bacura: Oh, hang on a second.

Mai: Scary.
Setton: See, you shouldn't have picked on him.
Setton: Now Bacura's gone silent.
Bacura: Oh, sorry.
Bacura: I'm going to fix some dinner for a bit.
Bacura: I'll be in the chat, I just won't be able to respond for a while.
Setton: Have fun.

<Private Mode> Bacura: There, that should buy me some time to focus on this convo.
<Private Mode> TarouTanaka: Very polite of you. Oh, it looks like you're fixing that habit of ending lines after every bit of punctuation.
<Private Mode> Bacura: At any rate, there's a reason that I want to talk to you as Mikado rather than TarouTanaka today. You could say I was waiting for you.
<Private Mode> TarouTanaka: You could just call me, you know. My number's the same.
<Private Mode> Bacura: No, I'll pass. I feel like my resolve will waver if I hear your voice right now.

Kuru: By the way, does anyone here have plans for their extended vacation coming up? We are surprisingly domestic, so we prefer to stay indoors and cherish our love.
Setton: Love? Are you and Mai married or something?
Mai: Secret.
Saika: i will be at home

<Private Mode> Bacura: I'm talking to Kuru and stuff, too.
<Private Mode> Bacura: Are you going anywhere for Golden Week?

Setton: I'm guessing I'll be playing video games with my partner.
Kuru: Oh, you have someone with whom to grow your love, too, Setton?
Mai: Together.
Setton: Er, uh, love... Well, I guess you could say that, lol.

Saika: love?

<Private Mode> TarouTanaka: No, I have no plans! So if you want to meet, I'm open!
<Private Mode> TarouTanaka: I know your dad is completely hands-off with you, so he might not care if you quit school, but everyone else is worried about you. Even Mr. Satou is concerned.
<Private Mode> TarouTanaka: Even Anri really wants to see you.
<Private Mode> Bacura: ...No, sorry, that's not what I'm talking about.

Kuru: If we were to leave, we'd probably just walk around Ikebukuro. Nothing more exciting than shopping at Parco and seeing a movie on Sixtieth Floor Street.
Mai: I want to see a movie.

<Private Mode> Bacura: You going anywhere during your extended vacation?
<Private Mode> TarouTanaka: Huh? No, I'm just going to school tomorrow for some student committee stuff.
<Private Mode> Bacura: I see... Listen, Mikado, this is a warning.
<Private Mode> Bacura: During your vacation, I wouldn't go out alone at night.
<Private Mode> Bacura: On top of that, don't get together with the other Dollars for a while.
<Private Mode> TarouTanaka: Huh?

Setton: Oh, but sometimes I wish I could go riding through the forests of my old home with my partner.
Kuru: Well, we have this vacation coming up. Why not take the opportunity to visit home?
Setton: Unfortunately, it's too much distance to just stop by.

<Private Mode> Bacura: Just be a normal high school student with no connection to the Dollars for a little while.
<Private Mode> TarouTanaka: What do you mean?

Setton: Are you going anywhere, Tarou?

* * *

<Private Mode> Bacura: I don't really know the specifics, so I can't go into any detail.
<Private Mode> Bacura: A hunch. Let's just say it's a hunch.
<Private Mode> Bacura: I have a bad feeling right now.
<Private Mode> Bacura: That the Dollars are in danger. Yes, a bad feeling that the Dollars are in danger.
<Private Mode> TarouTanaka: The Dollars are?
<Private Mode> TarouTanaka: All right, whatever's going on, I'll be careful.
<Private Mode> TarouTanaka: Your hunches are never wrong, Masaomi.

Setton: Oh, no response. He must be afk.
Setton: Oops, it looks like I've got a visitor, so I've got to go.
Kuru: Oh, I suppose that will be our parting for this evening. I am exceedingly sad to see you go, but I choose to savor the loneliness that is fate's work. For I am certain that I am not the only one to sip that bitter liquid now. Have a pleasant holiday, Setton.
Mai: Buh-byes, Setton.
Bacura: So long.
Saika: thank you
Setton: Saika, I haven't done anything that deserves thanks, lol.
Setton: At any rate, so long, everyone.
Setton: Night!

Setton has left the chat.

<Private Mode> Bacura: Thanks, Mikado.
<Private Mode> Bacura: Be careful.
<Private Mode> TarouTanaka: Thanks to you, too, Masaomi. Really, thanks for so much.
<Private Mode> Bacura: Don't be so formal.

Bacura: Well, folks, I've got some business to take care of. Gotta go for today.
Bacura: (>_<)ノシ

* * *

Bacura has left the chat.

Kuru: Good evening. May the true Kuroni City appear in your dreams.

TarouTanaka: Good night.
TarouTanaka: Huh? Setton's already left.
TarouTanaka: Oh no, now it looks like I totally ignored Setton.
TarouTanaka: I'm sorry.
Saika: i dont think setton minds
Kuru: Oh, what a twist of fate. At the start of this chat, TarouTanaka was beleaguered by the missing Setton, and now it is Tarou who has left Setton out to dry... What is it that the cyberspace purports to teach us, one wonders!
Mai: To love each other.
Kuru: I would appreciate it if you didn't respond out of mindless reflex, Mai.
Saika: love?
TarouTanaka: ...Gosh, I'm sorry.
TarouTanaka: That reminds me. Kanra didn't show up today.
Kuru: He is very busy with his wicked plottings. If only he were always wasting time in this chat room, the world would be a much more peaceful place.
Mai: Evil bastard.
Saika: kanra doesnt seem bad to me
TarouTanaka: Have you met Kanra in person, Saika?
Saika: only here, sorry
TarouTanaka: Well, I don't think he's a bad person, just a little eccentric.
Kuru: Alas, it seems that even here, we have more unfortunate souls taken in by Kanra's honeyed lies...

.

.

.

.

.

Interlude or Prologue A, Chikage Rokujou

May 3, night, Itabashi Ward, a certain place

On a pedestrian crossing bridge over Route 254, also known as the Kawagoe Highway, stood a young man wearing a medical eyepatch, surrounded by a flock of young women, watching the car lights coming and going below.

"Hey, Rocchi, does it still hurt?"

"It hurts like hell. But as long as I'm with you all, I feel amazing. The breath of hot girls is like an anesthetic that melts me into goo," Chikage said, rubbing the bandage on his cheek.

One of the girls looked at him with deadly seriousness. "Hey, Rocchi."

"What is it?"

"That's creepy."

"Wha…?!"

He stumbled and lurched as if he was traumatized but did not seem particularly upset. He smiled at the group of women.

"Listen, thanks for showing me around Ikebukuro today. It's been a huge help."

"It's totally fine, Rocchi. I know you've hardly ever left your hometown."

"But you scared me, the way you showed up so badly hurt like that!"

"You shouldn't get in over your head, Rocchi. You know you're bad at fighting."

Chikage grimaced at their comments and retorted, "No, I'm not."

"Did you win, then?"

"...No, I lost."

"See? I knew it."

The girls sighed. He grumbled back at them.

"Only because the other guy was way too tough. But it was the first real, straight-up fight I've had in ages. He turned out to be nicer than I thought, actually," he said wistfully.

The girls were not amused.

"I have no idea what that's supposed to mean." "Why would you fight him if he's so nice?" "Guys never grow out of being children..." "And you're *especially* childish, Rocchi..." "He's only adult below the waist..." "That's gross." "And who invites eight women out on a date at the same time?" "You know he actually asked about ten more?" "Most of them got mad and left." "Yeah, it's sickening." "Why are we even hanging out with this philanderer?" "Because we're weird?"

As the onslaught of chirped insults and slanders jabbed Chikage, he scowled and looked away.

"You girls say whatever comes to mind, don't you? Well, the other day I saw a thing on TV about a nobleman who loved, like, thirty different maids. At least I'm better than him, right?"

"Really? You said you were super-jealous of him."

"...Look, just forget about that. Take care on your way home. Stick together until you get to the train station," he said, eager to change the subject.

The girls rolled their eyes but gave him smiles.

"We know, we know. You're such a worrywart, Rocchi."

"So long."

And with that, the girls trotted away down the bridge.

After sending the girls off with a smile, the young man returned to gazing at the highway alone in the dark of night.

* * *

Chikage stood there silently for several minutes in the breeze. When he spoke at last, his monologue melted in the sound of the traffic below.

"Still, it's the first time I've been beaten to a pulp so solidly like that. And he even helped me get to a doctor. Total defeat. Weird doctor, though."

"You, losing in a fistfight? Go figure."

The voice came from straight behind the young man.

It was a rough, blunt man's voice, nothing like the chirping of the young women who had just been there.

Chikage did not turn to face the voice. He continued watching the lights of the city.

"Yeah… But he wasn't human. I never wanna fight him again."

"That dangerous?"

"Well, it was our guys who started it by picking a fight with him in the first place, so there's no need to do anything more. It's more of a selfish desire of mine."

"It's not like Heiwajima was our goal for coming here to start with."

"Yeah, exactly," Chikage chuckled. He spoke to the expanding aura gathering around him. "Shizuo Heiwajima was nothing more than a bonus. The ones we're about to face tonight are the real reason we're here."

He looked up slowly, pulling his eyes away from the center divider of the highway and looking around him at last.

He saw a lineup of familiar faces.

Glares.

A crowd of piercing glares shot through Chikage Rokujou.

But the hostility of all those eyes was not directed at Chikage himself.

There were a few dozen men all around in leather jackets and biker uniforms.

Despite being obviously underage, there was a powerful foreboding in the image that seeped into the air around them.

There were so many that they couldn't all fit on the walkway, so some of them gathered on the stairs and the sidewalk below.

Chikage Rokujou let himself fuse with the aura of the menacing group around him, his words growing sharper by the moment.

"An eye for an eye. A tooth for a tooth. An obligation for an obligation... If they play dirty, then we're more than happy to stoop to their level. It was our idiots who started it all by causing trouble in Ikebukuro, and I forced 'em to make things right...but what happened next ain't cool."

"Three more of us got knocked out yesterday. It was a total ambush," one of the young men reported.

"...*Tsk!* So I guess none of the rules apply with these guys, huh?" Chikage spat. He gritted his teeth—then grinned. "We ain't exactly saints, either... Who says we gotta play fair against pieces of shit like them?"

And Chikage Rokujou—leader of Toramaru, biker gang from Saitama—spoke with quiet menace of the dark emotions that ran through him.

"I understand wanting payback, but I take offense at their methods. Coming all the way to Saitama and ambushing not only *us*, but also *others who had nothing to do with anything.* If they'd stuck to just attacking our team, that would make sense, since we started it."

The leader stretched and cracked his neck before finally identifying their target.

"I don't know how people see 'em here...but it seems to me like these *Dollars* are a real sick bunch."

"It don't matter who these guys are," said one of his followers. Despite their leader's admission that he lost his fight, their resolve had not diminished in the least. These were not the ones who had gone on a joyride rampage through Ikebukuro—they were bound by firm determination and camaraderie.

"Well, these Dollars, or whatever stupid name they call themselves, are gonna find out what *we're* all about now," Chikage announced to his silent squad.

Dark flames began to burn within them, rising to face a singular purpose.

* * *

Revenge.

An unknown gang had ransacked their neighborhood.

Their pride had been crushed.

Perhaps their friends or family outside of the gang had been hurt.

Chikage Rokujou faced the crowd with thick rage waiting in its throat and uttered the words that unleashed the fury into the air.

"The Dollars are gonna get a lesson…about which gang is *truly crazy*!"

""""""RRRRRAAAAAAAHHHHH!""""""

A wave of roaring anger rippled through the night.

The gathering broke up at once, the members trickling into the night before they could draw more attention.

Chikage continued watching them from his spot on the bridge.

Unlike when he had fought Shizuo, he wore a truly cruel and villainous smile now.

"Oh, and I'm sure all the guys in my personal group know this already," he added, just in case.

"But anyone who hits a woman, Dollars or not…is gonna get his skull personally bashed in, courtesy of me. Keep that in mind."

The Black Market Doctor Gets Sappy, Part Two

Hey, Celty. Sorry about the wait.

It's been quite a rush around here, hasn't it?

It looks like you had to cut off your chat session. Is everything okay? I know you like checking in regularly. The chat room with that Saika girl, right?

Well, Shizuo just showed up out of the blue with this bloody kid in tow.

Seems like he had a fight.

Honestly, it's been ages since he'd actually brought me someone he hit himself.

Probably not since high school. At the time, emergency first aid was about the best I could do. You were out working at the time, I think.

Back then, I hardly ever told you about school, but it was actually pretty rough.

Shizuo and Izaya fought like dogs and cats from the moment I met them. Or more like…vampires and werewolves.

Speaking of which, have you ever met a real vampire or werewolf, Celty?

Oh, I see.

So there are all kinds, even when it comes to vampires and werewolves.

But you've hardly seen any vampires since coming to Japan. Well, that makes sense.

If anything, you're the most visible spooky thing around here.

...But you're still afraid of the Grays?

Uh, Celty? Celty?

Do you still believe the theory that the Grays were what wiped out the dinosaurs?

...

No, listen, Celty, the photon belt isn't some gigantic life-form. You realize that, right? I've never heard anyone before say, "We might get eaten by the photon belt."

...

No, no, no! We're not going to be overrun by beings from the fourth dimension!

Look! No matter how hard Yumasaki tries, a three-dimensional person cannot simply become two-dimensional! So it'd be similarly hard for a fourth-dimensional person to get here! It'll be fine! What? You're scared of tesseracts? Have you been reading that sci-fi manga again? That's not the same as reality!

It's funny how you don't mind ghosts or goblins in the least, but you cannot handle anything like aliens. You know, they always have those debate specials on TV, but you never see people who believe in ghosts but not in Venusians. I wish they would jump around more between pro and anti with that stuff.

...What did that TV show just remind you of?

...

It's fine! Nothing to be scared of with that prophecy!

Remember how nothing happened in 1999? So 2012 will be perfectly safe, too!

That reminds me, back in June of 1999, you were terrified by the thought that your missing head was the great king of terror prophesied by Nostradamus.

What? The Mayan calendar ends in 2012?

Then how far ahead should the Mayans have constructed their calendar?

The year 3000? The year 500,000,000?

How much work do you demand those poor Mayans do?! You have no idea how much work it took for them to create a year's worth of calendar! For that matter, neither do I.

On that note, the calendar in my pocket organizer only covers up to 2009. Are you going to start saying you're afraid of 2009 now, Celty?

Plus, you're not even considering the possibility that humanity could be wiped out by nuclear war or a meteorite before 2012 arrives.

If you'd spread that story around about the year 1800, people would probably have said, "That means we're totally safe until the year 2012! Yahoo!" And the rest would ignore you.

But most "prophets" are really just people who are skilled at taking very loose evidence and twisting it to suit their story. Not that I'm saying they *can't* be real.

Let's take…Izaya, for instance.

He has qualities that make him close to a prophet.

You know how he talks as though he can see through everything that's happening?

Whenever trouble arises, he wafts in afterward and acts like he caused it all—and then reaps the benefits after the fact. Even though he did nothing up to that point.

It's like when false prophets claim they foresaw actual events of the past, long before they happened. It's Izaya Orihara's style to get people to believe him when he says that.

In fact, if you treat him very calmly and rationally, the things he says aren't ordinarily believable… What he does is tell you the worst possible thing at the worst possible moment to rattle you and make you vulnerable.

If Izaya got on TV calling himself a prophet, he'd be quite a hit, I bet.

Though knowing him, once he found himself with a following of believers, he'd get bored, proclaim something about Japan sinking into the ocean, then disappear and leave chaos in his wake.

Ever since school, he was always good at leading people on.

That's what he was good at—leading people on, not out and out fooling them. He had a pointless knack for it.

And that's why my high school time was so miserable. Shizuo was ferocious, Izaya was fishy, and not a single girl wanted anything to do with me. Of course, I was living with you, so I didn't need any girls.

At any rate, you cannot let Izaya lead you astray. Unlike the false prophets, he doesn't have a shred of goodwill. Not that I would want to be told fake prophecies for a good cause.

Huh? What would I do if I were a true prophet who saw a future vision of the world destroyed?

...You do realize I was just talking very fervently about how Izaya in real life is more dangerous than any prophecy, right? Shall I assume you were just ignoring that whole part?

That makes me kind of sad, but I find that aspect of you endearing as well, so I'll let it slide.

If I could predict the future, and I knew that humanity could escape calamity through its actions as a whole, then I'd make, like, ten billion yen gambling, blow it up to a few trillion through the stock market, use the money to prove and publicize my powers of foresight, *then* tell everyone about the future. If that takes until there's only three days left until oblivion, I'll just give up and hold you tight instead!

...Weird. I figured that would be the point where you get overcome with emotion and leap into my arms.

You know, a proven prophet is something like a time machine when you think about it. It's like a time machine that can only send information from the future into the past.

...

Celty, please don't start talking about how scary an out-of-control AI would be.

It's so strange how you can be confident and brave, but as soon as the topic of aliens and the like comes up, you switch into scaredy-cat mode. It's super-cute, though!

...

...You're not going to pinch me or poke me with your shadow?

Look, I'm not a masochist or anything, but when you don't do your usual thing, it's a bit worrying for me…

"I'm calm now, thanks"?

You must have really been terrified.

It's fine; you can cry in my arms. Then, we'll go to bed. We can engage in some pillow tal— Ah-ah-ah-aah! That's a bit more like your usual sel-el-el-el-elf! Ouch! Ow…owww!

Ooh, that hurt. But I'm glad you're feeling better.

And just so you know, I'm not a skeptic of supernatural phenomena. I'm a proponent, if anything.

I mean, I have the miracle of your presence, Celty.

I called you spooky earlier, but I take that back now.

You're not a fairy or a goblin or a ghost.

You're a miracle of love.

It doesn't matter if you're a fairy, or a demon, or an angel to me.

As the saying goes, "You can find a fruitful tree by its flowers," but in your case, it would be more like "You can find the sweetness of honey by its dapple shade." From the moment I met you, I understood what an enchanting person you were! All on my own!

…Hmm?

Oh no, not now!

Sorry, Celty. The kid Shizuo brought here is awake.

I need to go explain the situation. Don't want him to go all berserk in here.

Whew, thanks for waiting.

He's up and walking now, so I sent him back home. Since Shizuo hit him, I told him about another unlicensed doctor working at a place that can actually do a brain scan. He'll need that kind of help.

It really is inconvenient not having, for example, an MRI machine. So I got this doctor's info from some people at Dad's company last month.

Speaking of Shizuo, he shouldn't be relying on me so heavily, just because I cut him a good deal.

He seems to think that our little love nest is a Red Cross tent.

It's an insult to all upstanding legitimate doctors to associate a black market doc like me with their work.

Speaking of which, have you ever had any war experience, Celty?

...

So your memory of that time is still vague.

You think it's in your head...? Come on, Celty. You can't start with the head search thing again.

As long as you're here in this city, you won't have any connection to war, I'd say.

As they say, Japan has gone soft from its peace, but I'm grateful for the conditions that created that softness. It just means things are quiet for you and me.

But you never know when that peace might come to an end, so we ought to foster as much love together while we still can!

So let's continue what we were— Er-er-er-er-ow-ow-ow-ow, ouch, ouch! That hurts! It hurts when you use your shadow to lock both my arms to-to-to-to-to— Give! Give, give! I give...!

Chapter 2

DRRR!! 5 NA9-30

Ryohgo Narita

THE ADULTS SQUIRM

May 3, Ikebukuro

Right around the time that Shizuo Heiwajima was being hit with a stun gun by an unidentified little girl, Celty Sturluson was herself thrust into the midst of the abnormal.

But in her case, it was part of her job.

Gone soft from peace, huh?

She leaned back into the pleasantly textured sofa, thinking about what her partner had said the night before.

That seems like the kind of thing that would never describe a black market doctor and a courier.

She was sitting in what might seem at first glance like a neatly arranged office.

But the interior of the office was exceedingly minimalistic, with just the barest necessities when it came to furniture. She understood that this was so the office could be closed up and removed at a moment's notice or to allow it to be morphed into a different tenant altogether.

And such an occurrence would only happen when the police started to move in.

"We appreciate you taking the time to come visit today. Would you like a hot towel to clean off?"

"Oh, don't mind me," Celty typed into her PDA, turning her attention to the man sitting across from her. He was around thirty years of age, and his name was Shiki.

This man brought Shinra a number of clients and had hired Celty to ferry around things on several occasions.

To outward appearances, he was the representative of a small art dealership—but as a matter of fact, he was only a member of a much larger group. In truth, he was an officer of a group of *professional gentlemen* known as the Awakusu-kai, working for the Medei-gumi Syndicate.

The art dealership's office was merely a front for the group. In fact, there wasn't even a single painting hanging up in the waiting room.

"I understand the desire to have some art on display just for appearances, but I can't seem to acquire anything that suits my aesthetic," Celty recalled the man saying once, but it meant nothing to her.

More concerning was the fact that whenever a new person entered the office, he would invariably tense up when he saw Celty.

"Um...I can't help noticing some tension from the group."

"Hmm? Oh, pardon them. There was someone dressed similarly to you in the office of our syndicate's money-lending business the other day. They had some rather...rough words of complaint, shall we say."

At the moment, Celty was wearing her black riding suit with the full helmet. She understood his meaning, was fed up with it, and typed, *"Shall I change outfits?"*

Fortunately, at times like these there was no way for them to see how weary she felt.

"No, you don't need to feel so weary."

Is he psychic?!

"Can you read my mind?"

"All you have to do is watch the subtle mannerisms. Any man who can't pick up that sort of information without a face to read isn't cut out for this line of work. Oh, but feel free to change. You could even remove your helmet if you want."

...

"Are you certain?"

"Sure. Most people take theirs off when they go indoors."

"You do know...what I am, don't you?"

"Go ahead," Shiki said, his gaze unflinching. Taken aback, Celty grabbed her helmet and lifted it straight off the base of her neck.

The next instant, the other few men present in the room froze still, and a young "employee" who happened to be passing nearby flinched and yelped, "Wha—?! M-monst…"

Instantly, Shiki leaped from the sofa and grabbed the young man by the collar. Without listening for an excuse, he rammed the man's face into the corner of a nearby locker.

"Gahk!" the young man grunted, blood flowing from his mouth.

Shiki lifted the man by the collar, pressed his forehead against the man's temple, and said flatly, "What kind of a man screams when he sees his guest's face?"

"Agh…blrgh…"

"What did I just say? I just said that most people take their helmets off when they go indoors."

"Um, wait," Celty hurriedly typed into her PDA, confused at what was going on, but naturally Shiki was not looking in her direction and did not see the message.

"So why would my subordinate scream at her, after I just told my guest she could take her helmet off?"

"…S…szorry…szir…," the younger man gurgled.

Shiki smiled coldly at him. "You're apologizing to the wrong person. Why would you say sorry to me?"

Shiki was about to deliver another devastating blow when a black shadow twisted around his arm.

A literal shadow.

A shadow with mass, occupying three-dimensional space, writhing through the air like a tentacle to grab Shiki's hand and hold it in place.

"…"

He turned around to see a freshly typed message on the PDA screen.

"Look, I'm not offended."

The PDA screen with its large message was propped up by a different shadow from the one holding Shiki's arm still. In fact, countless shadows were extending from Celty's hands, much to the shock of the other employees watching the scene. Given what Shiki had just done to their cohort, they wisely held their silence.

Shiki slowly lowered himself into a chair, smiling as though nothing had happened, and said, "I see. I'm afraid we've presented a rather embarrassing spectacle."

"Not at all."

...These people really are scary. It's just a different kind of scary from the motorcycle cops.

"I apologize for the disrespect. I was the one who offered you the opportunity to take off your helmet, but it seems my man here did not understand the meaning of my statement," Shiki said, bowing deeply.

Celty felt a chilling pressure emanating from him. *But...I'm pretty sure it's the first time I've ever taken it off around him, too.*

True, this was the first occasion that the man named Shiki had ever seen what was under Celty's helmet. But there was no panic or change in his expression. He hadn't even taken an extra breath. Celty found that to be quite eerie.

Having that part of me totally ignored actually puts extra pressure on me...

To Celty, the screaming reaction of the young man now holding his broken nose and bowing was the normal one for a human being.

Because it wasn't the physical shadows extending from her fingertips that was the eeriest part of the picture.

It was the fact that underneath her helmet, *there was no head atop her shoulders.*

♂♀

Celty Sturluson was not human.

She was a type of fairy commonly known as a dullahan, found from Scotland to Ireland—a being that visits the homes of those close to death to inform them of their impending mortality.

The dullahan carried its own severed head under its arm, rode on a two-wheeled carriage called a Coiste Bodhar pulled by a headless horse, and approached the homes of the soon to die. Anyone foolish enough to open the door was drenched with a basin full of blood. Thus, the dullahan, like the banshee, made its name as a herald of ill fortune throughout European folklore.

One theory claimed that the dullahan bore a strong resemblance to the Norse Valkyrie, but Celty had no way of knowing if this was true.

It wasn't that she *didn't* know. More accurately, she just couldn't remember.

When someone back in her homeland stole her head, she lost her memories of what she was. It was the search for the faint trail of her head that had brought her here to Ikebukuro.

Now with a motorcycle instead of a headless horse and a riding suit instead of armor, she had wandered the streets of this neighborhood for decades.

But ultimately, she had not succeeded in retrieving her head, and her memories were still lost.

Celty knew who stole her head.

She knew who was preventing her from finding it.

But ultimately, that meant she didn't know where it was.

And she was fine with that.

As long as she could live with those human beings she loved and who accepted her, she could happily go on the way she was now.

She was a headless woman who let her actions speak for her missing face and held this strong, secret desire within her heart.

That was Celty Sturluson in a nutshell.

♂♀

Now this headless fairy rode all over Ikebukuro as a lowly courier, taking on odd jobs from a variety of people, paying no mind to whether the job was aboveboard or under the table.

In this case, it was clear that the job she was being hired for was way, way under the table.

"Sorry about him. He was working in debt collection for a financial agent of ours until recently, when he was reassigned to our wing for being a little too loud and a little too inefficient at his job."

"Debt collection? You mean like what Shizuo does?" Celty wrote on a whim and then froze, realizing her mistake.

Shizuo would not take to a job of this sort. The thought of what might happen if Shiki's organization honestly tried to recruit him sent a shiver down her back.

But Shiki's response was surprisingly aloof.

"Shizuo… Oh, him."

Shiki already knew about Shizuo Heiwajima. He looked away.

"He does collection for a call-girl service, right? They won't have any connection to a business like ours. I did hear about some idiot borrowing money from us who also tried to shirk his debt to the call service and wound up in a heap of trouble."

"I see."

"…Do you really think any loan shark wants to use a well-known troublemaker widely recognized by the police for a collection bruiser?"

"I do not," she had to admit.

In that light, she also had to admit that his dreadlocked boss must be quite skilled at handling Shizuo to keep him from getting into trouble with the police.

"But enough about him. Let's get down to business," Shiki said, pulling a photograph from his pocket. "This is not so much of a courier job…but a more unique request, much like the earlier job involving retrieving materials."

"I see."

Celty recalled another job she'd taken from this man about a year earlier. Some men who stole a gun were on the run, and they needed her to retrieve it before the police could and bring it back.

It wasn't the kind of job she wanted to do, but when she learned that the thieves were the type to point a gun at innocent civilians, and given that she owed the Awakusu-kai a number of large debts from when she first came to Japan, she had no choice but to accept the job.

At the time, I tried to slip the gun to the police by pretending I failed to get it back, but this man showed up first…

Shiki was not a man to be underestimated, and this job would require careful consideration before she accepted. Her own well-being was one thing, but if the job threatened to affect Shinra and the other people of Ikebukuro she knew like Mikado, Anri, Shizuo, and Kadota in a negative way, she had to consider those consequences very heavily before accepting or declining.

Warily, she reached out to accept the photo. Examining it through her unique visual sense that involved no eyeballs, she saw a middle-aged man.

He looked to be somewhere from his midforties to early fifties. In the photo he was smiling in a friendly, gentlemanly way. There were reading glasses on his nose, and his outfit was formal, giving him the appearance of a company president, or perhaps the chairman of a private academy.

Who is this? I hope he's not going to ask me to kill him.

For a brief moment she was going to type her statement about killing the man, but the thought occurred to her that the man might be a higher-up in the yakuza syndicate, so she stuck to a simple question.

"Who is this man?"

"Jinnai Yodogiri. The fellow who was representative director of Yodogiri Shining Corporation… Perhaps you've heard of them?"

Oh! From Ruri Hijiribe!

"Yes, I know."

Ruri Hijiribe was the name of a massive star, an up-and-coming actress who had recently caused a stir when her relationship with male star Yuuhei Hanejima was exposed in the tabloids. She was a true actor's actor, and both Celty and Shinra eagerly followed her career.

With the revelation of that affair came another bit of personal trouble.

Jinnai Yodogiri, president of her talent agency, Yodogiri Shining Corporation, went missing under mysterious circumstances, effectively releasing all of the agency's talent into the wild. Without anywhere else to go, she found herself enrolled with Jack-o'-Lantern Japan, the agency representing Yuuhei Hanejima.

Rumor said that she got in because of the good word of her paramour, Hanejima, but the disappearance of the agency head was given bigger headlines, and after a month, the whole affair was in the process of being forgotten by society at large.

"So what happened to this showbiz president?" Celty asked.

Shiki tapped his right index finger on the desk. "As a matter of fact, we had our own personal dealings with him…and there were some differences of opinion between us."

"Ah."

"Naturally, we are doing our best with our own resources to search for him…but we could use all the help we can get right now. I'm not asking you to spend all your time on this, but given your job as a courier, you meet people from many walks of life. I was hoping you might be able to let us know about any information you come across..."

"I don't know if I'll be any help to you there."

But even then, is this the kind of thing they'd call me for? And if I do somehow find him and let them know, I have a feeling this Yodogiri fellow will wind up feeding the worms in the mountains or the fish at the bottom of the sea.

Seeing that she was hesitant about the idea, Shiki smiled wryly and added, "Only if you happen to come across anything. There's no need to overanalyze it."

He saw through me again, she realized, suspicious. Based on the way he was talking, there naturally had to be some other job he wanted to ask her about.

"The thing is...there's another thing we wanted to ask of you..."

"This also has little to do with your courier job..."

♂♀

May 3, evening, near Kawagoe Highway, apartment building

Ahhh, I wish Celty would come back soon.

It was the luxury apartment where the headless fairy and her human companion lived.

In the midst of this vast living space, boasting over fifteen hundred square feet and five bedrooms, Shinra Kishitani was lounging atop a rug, waiting for his beloved to return home.

He was wearing his white doctor's coat as he rolled idly on the floor, which only made him look like a weirdo. As a matter of fact, there was another white coat wrapped in plastic in the corner of the room, meaning that he had separate doctors' coats for work and private wear.

But just the idea of wearing a doctor's lab coat for a personal outfit was weird enough to begin with.

Shinra was a black market doctor who took in patients who couldn't see an ordinary doctor for various reasons. But as he didn't have X-rays or other fancy machinery, he was not in high demand.

Yet because he was a flexible freelancer, he did have certain regular clients. If he wanted to have a normal, upstanding position, he had the ability, the knowledge, and the qualifications. But he did not want that—he preferred to live his life dishonestly and spend his days with Celty.

She's getting a job from Shiki. It's odd because she tries not to take on jobs from those sorts nowadays. It was much less of a problem for her when she didn't really care about humans. But I think Mr. Shiki understands that about her now.

Shinra did not think of Shiki as being good-hearted—he was a man who lived firmly on the underside of society. But because he was so familiar with what it took to do his work, he wouldn't send the *darker* jobs to someone like her, whose personal morals were wavering.

He needed the right person for every job.

Shiki would send such work to others, people who were more predictable in their outlook. Shinra was reassured that Celty would be fine because he knew Shiki to be a pragmatic man at heart.

Of course, it was best not to associate with such people at all, but as Celty was not even human to begin with, she didn't have the luxury of being picky about her income sources.

She's the type of girl who would keep working a job for a sense of fulfillment, even after winning three hundred million yen in the lottery.

...If we had a baby, I wonder if she'd give up her job to be a housewife. I suppose I should find out if it's even possible for us to have children first.

We could also take in a foster child. On the forms, it'd have to go down as Dad and my stepmother's child.

Wait...I just envisioned myself as a househusband while Celty goes out and works.

Celty as a housewife... With an apron...made of shadow.

What? She's naked under the apron?!

He rolled even harder on the rug, grinning at the image in his head. Shinra looked like nothing short of a freak, but his partner was nowhere in sight to make fun of him.

* * *

After spending about thirty minutes like that, the doorbell rang.

"Ooh! Is she back?" he wondered aloud, hopping up excitedly. The doorbell rang several more times as he raced over to the entryway.

"I wonder why she's ringing the bell. Did she forget her key?"

He was so preoccupied with the thought of Celty that the possibility of anyone else being responsible for ringing the doorbell never even entered his mind.

He realized his mistake right as he was reaching the door, but it was too late to stop. When he opened it, he saw the very same bartender uniform he'd seen just last night.

"..."

At least it wasn't a gun-toting hit man or a home invader, but in terms of potential danger, this visitor was a good match.

Shinra closed the door halfway and groaned. "Maybe I should move to a building that won't even let you in the front entrance without a key."

"Sounds to me like you wanna get socked," Shizuo said.

Shinra grimaced and waved his hand. "Please don't. Then I'd have to consider the very real possibility that I would die."

"Can I come in?" Shinra's longtime acquaintance mumbled, scratching his cheek.

The doctor said, "Fine, fine. What is it now? The kid you brought here yesterday already left; he was in good enough shape to walk again."

"Yeah, I know. He was in town earlier, I hear."

"Very lively fellow. Especially after taking several hits from you. It's a wonder all his vertebrae were still in place," Shinra noted, pulling the door back open to usher Shizuo inside, when he noticed—

"Huh?"

Shizuo was not the only person outside the apartment.

"Huh? Isn't that your boss...?"

"Yeah, I've never introduced you two. This is Tom."

"Yes, I understand that, but..."

Shinra was not looking at the man with the dreadlocks—but at a little girl of around elementary school age, clinging to Shizuo's waist by his belt.

* * *

"Who's the girl?"

♂♀

At that moment, Raira Academy

Whether private school or public school, vacation is vacation.

Like the rest of society, the private Raira Academy, famous for its close proximity to Ikebukuro Station, was in the first day of the extended break.

But the school was overflowing with more people than one would expect. The athletic clubs were crowded onto the field, bellowing to be heard over the others, and the humanities clubs were each busy preparing for their artistic contests in June.

Mikado Ryuugamine was one of these students on campus during the break. He was considered a member of the Going Home club, as he didn't participate in any extracurriculars. Instead, he was here for a student committee meeting about the class field trip.

Normally, this would have happened after school, but the meetings had been running long, and so they had to make it up by holding an extra one during the break. The school was reluctant, but since it was the students' idea, the plan was approved to hold the meeting on campus during break and finalize plans once they'd collected the feedback of those class representatives who weren't able to make it due to vacation plans.

"Whew, finally done," Mikado groaned. He hadn't expected that planning their own field trip would involve such fierce debate.

From over his shoulder a tiny voice called, "Nice work, Mikado."

"Ah, Sonohara. Wasn't that tiring?"

Standing behind him was Anri Sonohara, his classmate and fellow representative on the student committee. But he had known her well before that—they met on the day they started school here.

Mikado's crush on Anri never left his own lips but was taken as public fact by everyone else, and Anri often interacted with Mikado, so the school essentially treated them like an official couple.

But neither Mikado nor Anri was aware of that. All they knew was that they were still friends, nothing more.

A part of Mikado wanted to confess his feelings and broach that gap, but another part of him wouldn't let that happen until a different problem was resolved.

He envisioned the face of his close friend who had recently quit school: Masaomi Kida.

They grew up in the same town, and with the addition of Anri in high school, they led a fulfilling school life.

The problem was, each of the three kept a terrible secret.

Mikado Ryuugamine, founder of the street gang the Dollars.

Masaomi Kida, founder and leader of a rival gang, the Yellow Scarves.

And Anri Sonohara, a girl who bore within her an inhuman *being* much like Celty Sturluson.

After a recent incident, the three each learned a bit about the others' secrets—and as a result, Masaomi Kida had left.

But neither Mikado nor Anri thought of this as a good-bye. They trusted that he would return, and therefore, neither attempted to pry into each other's half-exposed secrets.

They would speak openly when Masaomi came back to them. That was what they decided.

And thus, the relationship between the two neither progressed nor collapsed but maintained an awkward balance as the days passed them by.

Until yesterday, when a new event threatened to topple that balance.

In the chat room where Mikado went by the name TarouTanaka and Masaomi went by the handle Bacura, Masaomi reached out to speak not to TarouTanaka, but personally to Mikado Ryuugamine.

But should I tell Sonohara about that?

It was too menacing a topic to serve as a wholesome reunion with Masaomi.

The Dollars were in danger.

Curious and worried, Mikado checked out the mobile-only chat room and message board for Dollars members but found no particular evidence of the claim.

But it was true that when it came to such matters, Masaomi had a sharper instinct and deeper connections than himself.

If he just outright told Anri, it might only cause her to worry. Or was it better to just be open and explain the situation to her?

He walked through the school building with Anri, unsure of how to proceed, when an excited voice entirely at odds with his own mental state rang out.

"Mr. Mikado! Ms. Sonohara! Nice to see you!"

They turned around to see a boy in the hall: Aoba Kuronuma.

He was new, freshly enrolled just last month, their junior at school.

Aoba looked even younger than Mikado, to the point that he could pass himself off as an elementary schooler if he dressed the part. He could also pass for a girl if he cross-dressed and didn't speak.

He, too, was a member of the Dollars, one of the few who knew that Mikado was a fellow member—but since being dragged into a spot of trouble with Mikado and Anri last month, he hadn't made any major contact with them.

"Hi, Aoba… What's going on? First-years don't go on the field trip, right?" Mikado asked. He was certain that Aoba had been traumatized by their recent experience and was avoiding him as a result, but the boy's expression showed no sign of that—it was the same smile he'd seen a month earlier.

In fact, it was a little *too* carefree given that a violent biker gang had chased them—but Mikado Ryuugamine did not pick up on that.

"Nah, I'm here for my club. I'm in the art club."

"Oh, I didn't know that."

Was he here just for a little chat? Mikado prepared to respond appropriately. But before he could ask anything else, Aoba cut straight to the point.

"Are you free tomorrow?"

"Huh?"

"After what happened last month, you never got the chance to show me around the area! Since we have this extended break now, I thought the three of us could hang out for a day!"

"Er, well…tomorrow's not…"

Normally, Mikado would have agreed on the spot. But Masaomi's statement from the day before was bugging him.

"Don't get together with the other Dollars for a while," he had warned. Karisawa and Yumasaki were one thing, but did it really apply to Aoba Kuronuma?

Masaomi had said to just be a normal high schooler. And if he and Aoba didn't talk about the Dollars, they really were nothing more than students at the same school.

Maybe it would be safest to just not go out? If something might happen to the Dollars, maybe I should stay home and try to gather intelligence so I can send a warning message to everyone. Okay, I'll turn him down for now and make the offer again once this issue Masaomi mentioned dies down. I'd like to introduce Aoba to Masaomi, anyway.

After thinking it all through in his mind, Mikado shook his head sadly.

"Yeah… Sorry, I think I might have something going on tomorrow."

"Aww, darn," Aoba said, crestfallen. Right after, he picked his head up again and looked over at Anri. "What about you, Ms. Sonohara?"

"Huh? Me? I don't really have anything to do…"

What?

Mikado was at a total loss for words.

"But I won't be a very good tour guide…"

"Oh, it's fine! I did some groundwork of my own, looking stuff up!"

"But I doubt I'll be anything other than a bother to you."

…What? What?!

If Mikado and Anri had officially been a romantic couple, or if Anri were a bit quicker and more observant of others' feelings, she might not have reacted in the same way.

But since she was on the slow side when it came to recognizing *normal* romantic advances, she had no suspicions about what Aoba was asking her. She honestly wondered if he really thought she would be a good tour guide.

"That's not true! Ms. Anri, you're so beautiful, just having you around will make everything shine!"

Ms. Anri?! He's already leveled up from calling her by her last name?! Without checking first?! That's cheating! You're a cheater, Aoba!

"P-please, don't tease me."

"No, I'm serious. So what time should I—?"

At that point, Mikado spoke up. He made the mistake of speaking up.

"Wait! Whoopsie, I got myself mixed up. Tomorrow's open after all!"

"Oh, really?!" Aoba exclaimed, beaming innocently. That threw Mikado for a loop.

Wait...he's happy about that?

So he really was just teasing Sonohara?

"But only during the day. All kinds of people come out at night when school's out, and it gets dangerous after that."

"Yeah, sure thing," the boy said, his intentions still unreadable to Mikado.

And so it was that he made unexpected plans for the afternoon of the fourth. Or perhaps it would be more accurate to say that the plans were made for him.

Once again, Mikado would find himself stepping into the extraordinary—without knowing whether this was a product of simple coincidence or the intentions of someone else.

Perhaps he had been stepping across that line ever since the moment he founded the Dollars. He just didn't realize it.

Mikado Ryuugamine's ordinary life was coming to a quiet, unheralded end.

♂♀

Near Kawagoe Highway, apartment building

Shizuo sat on a sofa in the living room, drinking tea from a steel cup. He wondered, "So, Shinra...you even wear the lab coat at home?"

It was a perfectly natural question. Shinra puffed out his chest in mysterious pride and boasted, "Yes, because Celty's always dressed in her black riding suit, of course. The stark contrast makes us look like light and shadow, right? Light and shadow are polar opposites but always attached—a hot couple, just like us! When they talk about the forces of darkness in comics and movies, it's all just because the dark side is playing hard to get. Or maybe I'm just being possessive. To be honest, I wouldn't mind being possessed by Cel-*twah*!"

"Shut up."

Shizuo merely flicked Shinra's forehead with his finger, but the doctor flew backward as though a blunt weapon had struck him.

"I don't like your insinuation that you're on the side of light. You're way deeper on the dark side than Celty is."

"If you want to be peaceful like your name suggests, try limiting your feedback to words alone."

Meanwhile, Tom revealed his initial impression of the doctor under his breath. "Yeah, this guy really is a freak..."

"Hey! What do you mean, 'really is'? What kind of awful slander has Shizuo been spreading around the workplace about me?! Well...either way, I don't care. If talking about my love for Celty makes me a pervert, then a pervert I shall be. There's a thin line between perversion and love!" Shinra boasted, holding his swollen, reddening forehead. He slowed down to gather his breath and asked, "Anyway, would you mind explaining about her already?"

He looked over at the little girl curled up in the corner with her arms around her knees.

"You hushed me up earlier when you brought her in, but you realize I can't just ignore this, right? She looks scared out of her mind."

Shinra let out a very long, deep sigh and fixed his old friend with a stern gaze.

"Why did you kidnap her?"

"We didn't!" stated Tom.

He must have sensed that Shizuo was ready to snap and stepped in to deny it before anything happened. Sure enough, there was a vein bulging on Shizuo's face, but it was in the process of easing as the blood flow returned.

Tom shot the relieved Shinra a glance to warn him not to utter any more provocation before explaining the situation.

♂♀

Thirty minutes earlier, Sunshine, Sixtieth Floor Street

"Drop dead."

* * *

Huh?

Shizuo was on the tall side, so at first he couldn't be certain of what the little girl said when she leaped onto him.

If anything, Tom heard her better than Shizuo did, his expression one of disbelief as he rushed to catch up. But Tom's ears were working perfectly.

The girl thrust what she was holding against Shizuo's waist, never letting her smile fade away.

Tom saw a pale-blue spark leap from the tool to Shizuo's side, accompanied by a loud crackling sound.

"Yeow!" Shizuo yelped, instinctually brushing the girl's hand away.

"Ah!" she cried, as a boxy tool that looked like a transceiver fell from her grip.

Shizuo hadn't realized what had happened, and because he didn't process it, he also didn't instantly lose his temper like he usually did. Instead, he reached down to pick up what the girl dropped and examined it.

The black rectangular object looked like a walkie-talkie or a flashlight.

"...Damn, that hurt... What's going on? What is this?"

There was a switch on the device, so he pressed it.

It crackled and burst, and a blue spark leaped from the metallic part at the end of the device.

"What's this? A stun gun?"

He stood there in disbelief, his brain unable to process the combination of young girl and stun gun, when over his shoulder, Tom's voice caused him to come to his senses.

"Hey, Shizuo..."

All around them, pedestrians stopped in their tracks, looking over to see what was happening.

A grown man holding a stun gun.

A little girl on her knees next to him.

Right as he was able to process how the scene looked to an objective onlooker, one of those very people from the crowd started running over to a police officer stationed outside of the arcade.

"Oh, crap. It's the cop who came to arrest that shoplifter," Tom said and grabbed Shizuo's shoulder.

"We gotta go. You can't talk yourself out of this situation."

No sooner were the words out of his mouth than Tom began to utilize the sprinting power he'd gained since he started working with Shizuo.

"...Wh-whaa—?"

Shizuo had no choice but to follow his coworker, the opportunity to fly into a rage completely gone now.

They should have gotten away, and the police should've found the strange girl and taken her into custody.

Instead, Shizuo realized that he felt heavier than usual as he was running. He turned back and noticed a bob of flapping hair out of the corner of his eye.

Shizuo's monstrous strength was such that he never even noticed that the girl from a moment ago was clinging to his belt, dangling from his waist as he ran away from the scene.

"Can't run...away... Die...just...die...!" the little girl grunted as she clung to Shizuo.

He didn't understand what she was saying. He simply couldn't imagine a scenario in which a little girl would be trying to kill him.

One time after having been shot, he remained calm until he belatedly realized the attack was intentionally malicious. This was similar to that situation.

"So what should we do about her, Tom?" he asked as they ran. Tom glanced over, saw the girl on Shizuo's back, and shouted, "Arrgh, this is a nightmare!"

A moment later, he regained his cool and asked, "Do you know anyone who lives around here?! We're gonna stick out like a sore thumb on the street!"

"Our office?"

"No, we can't get our workplace involved! Oh, how about your brother's place?!"

"He's always getting staked out by reporters and tabloids."

Eventually, a single face popped into Shizuo's mind.

* * *

"...If you don't mind a black market doctor, there's one we can drag into this."

♂♀

"All right, I understand the situation now... For starters, I just have one thing to say," Shinra said calmly after they finished telling the story. He fixed Shizuo with a level gaze.

"Why did you kidnap her?!"

Krunkl.

Shinra looked over to see the source of the odd noise and saw Shizuo's clenched fist. Oddly, the steel cup that he'd been holding had vanished.

But the question was answered as quickly as it popped into his head. Shizuo opened his hand to reveal the object that had previously been a cup, crumpled into a ball like aluminum foil.

"Sorry. I'll pay you back."

"...No worries. I was just thinking about getting a new set."

"No, I feel sorry for the manufacturers who made this cup."

"Ah, if only you held the same regret in your heart for the poor guardrails and streetlights that you so frequently destroy—and as I'm saying that, I apologize for bringing that up—I'm so sorry. Of course you wouldn't kidnap her. If you were going to stoop to that level for money, it'd be a lot quicker to just pry open a bank safe with your bare hands."

Shinra looked over at the corner of the room with sweat trickling down his back. He noticed that the motionless little girl was trembling now.

"And you haven't gotten any info out of her?"

"That's the thing—she just keeps trembling like that. I know she was playing a dirty prank with this toy, but it still seems cruel to press her for answers," Shizuo replied, tossing the stun gun to Shinra.

He caught the tool and muttered in relief, "I'm glad to know you at least have some human sentiment in your heart. It would be completely indefensible to beat a poor little child like this."

The doctor walked over to the girl and crouched down to his knees to meet her eye level. "Are you all right? You're safe now. It must have been hard, being dragged around by those big, scary guys. You can relax; I'm a man of love and peace, not like that weapon in human form."

In the background, Tom was muttering to Shizuo, "Take it easy. The kid's watching, okay? Okay?"

Meanwhile, Shinra favored the girl with a disarming smile.

"…"

But she was totally silent, glaring back at him in distrust. She put up a brave front, but the trembling was quite severe. In fact, for having told him to "drop dead" and not once attempting to run away, the girl seemed remarkably passive.

"…"

Sensing something odd about her reaction, Shinra reached out to touch the girl's forehead. Instantly, the doctor's expression tightened, and he ordered the two men, "Go into the closet in that room over there and pull out the guest blankets!"

"?"

"She's burning up! We need to boil some water!"

With that, the apartment suddenly got very lively.

Whatever this change of heart in Shinra did to the girl, it caused her brittle tension to snap all at once, and she slumped over, completely unconscious.

♂♀

Thirty minutes later

With the girl slumbering away on a bed in the back, Shinra finally sighed in relief.

He didn't detect any signs of disease and came to the conclusion that it was probably just extreme tension and exhaustion, but you couldn't be too careful.

He stood in front of a hidden cabinet and pored over a selection of prescription-only medications before noticing the presence of a weight in his pocket. He pulled out the stun gun that Shizuo had tossed to him during the earlier scene.

Shinra switched it on again, causing another bolt of electricity and loud crackle. The sight of the clearly altered stun gun's effects brought the story of its use back to his mind.

"This thing's clearly been upgraded to boost its output..."

"...And he took a shot from it and only said, 'Yeow'? The guy really is turning into a monster."

♂♀

May 3, night, on the streets of Ikebukuro

Ahh, geez, Celty Sturluson lamented, trying to collect her thoughts. *I took on a real pain of a job this time.*

Celty was uncharacteristically gloomy in the midst of whatever job it was Shiki had given her. She was waiting at a stoplight on her lightless motorcycle, which emitted an engine roar that sounded oddly like whinnying.

Thanks, Shooter.

She stroked her partner's handlebars, grinning inwardly.

...If this doesn't go just right, I might not be home for several days. Maybe I should get in touch with Shinra now, while I have the chance. Either that or go home briefly to explain in person...

She noticed the signal for the cross street turn red. Celty waited on the left side of the two-lane road for the light to turn green, ready to send Shooter forward—but before the light changed, she sensed another motorcycle stop behind her.

Celty froze momentarily, terrified that it might be the usual cop, but when she trained her sense of vision backward, she saw that it was just an ordinary bike.

The rider had a full helmet like Celty's and wore a black riding suit. It was the prototypical outfit of a high-speed biker, and Celty did not think anything of it—until her visual senses picked up something odd.

...?

Before she could process what was wrong, the light turned green, and she automatically started driving.

"Good evening, Halloween Knight," the rear rider abruptly muttered.

Celty only heard it because of her heightened senses. It was probably meant for no ears but the speaker's.

She picked up speed, not knowing what to make of the comment.

"Playtime is over. Too bad, very sad."

Celty heard something resembling that coming from behind, and right at that moment—

A fierce shock ran through Celty's torso.

She felt her body slam onto the road but had no idea what was happening.

"This is a bodyguard job."

Through the dull pain, Celty heard what Shiki had told her earlier in the day.

"We don't know where the target is now..."

"But in short, we need you to find and protect a certain target in secret."

She'd had a bad feeling about it. Why ask *her* for protection?

But she couldn't turn down the job.

"...Her life might be targeted right now. I'm afraid I can't tell you much more than that..."

"I just want you to protect the person in this photograph."

He showed her a picture. It was of a little girl, maybe ten years old at best.

Her expression was gloomy, but she was putting on a happy face for the camera.

"Her name is Akane Awakusu."

"...She's the granddaughter of our 'company president.'"

"She's currently running away from home. She doesn't seem to approve of our 'business model.'"

It's not as if I like it, either, Celty thought. The pain came after a delay, bringing with it the confirmation that her bad feeling about this was correct.

She still couldn't tell what had happened to her.

But clearly *something* had, and that was all she needed to know.

She had confirmed two very crucial facts.

Number one—the shock of the impact had knocked her helmet high into the air.

Number two—she was getting herself into some very bad business.

And so it was that Celty, the most unrealistic of beings, was forcibly entangled with the reality of humankind.

May 3, night, chat room

TarouTanaka has entered the chat.

TarouTanaka: Good evening.
TarouTanaka: Nobody's around, looks like. Maybe they're all out?
TarouTanaka: I know I showed up late, but if even Setton isn't here...

Kuru has entered the chat.
Mai has entered the chat.

Mai: Good evening.
Kuru: And a most pleasant night to you, Tarou. Jumping right to the chat room on the first night of a vacation seems rather lonely to me, but on the other hand, the cyberspace realm knows no concepts such as vacations, holidays, day, or night. No one will condemn you here. But if you wish to be condemned, I can most certainly fulfill that role for you. The time has come to test whether you are the S or the M in S and M!
TarouTanaka: Oh, good evening.
TarouTanaka: Looks like you're still the same.
Kuru: The time has come to be tested!
TarouTanaka: Why did you say that twice?
Mai: Sorry.
TarouTanaka: And why are you apologizing?

Saika has entered the chat.

TarouTanaka: Ah, good evening.
Mai: Good evening.
Kuru: Well, well, another wandering traveler on a day off. Spending your vacation all at home will prove to be fatal. It is a superstition that a rabbit will die of loneliness, but it really does happen to people.
Saika: i'm sorry
TarouTanaka: Why are you apologizing, Saika? lol
Kuru: ...I don't know how to respond to that.

TarouTanaka: No wonder, because you've done nothing to require an apology.

Saika: i'm sorry

TarouTanaka: Again?!

TarouTanaka: And what does this say about you, Kuru?

TarouTanaka: You're here, too, aren't you?

Kuru: No need to worry. Mai and I ventured out into the streets of Ikebukuro to savor the heady taste of life. After first destroying all the gyoza at Namja Town's Gyoza Stadium, we enjoyed some shopping at World Import Mart and the Alpa mall, followed by the sight of a dashing gentleman stopping a robber along Sixtieth Floor Street.

Mai: The gyoza was yummy.

TarouTanaka: A robber? That sounds like quite a scene.

TarouTanaka: ...If it was on Sixtieth Floor Street, was it either a black man advertising for a sushi shop or a man in a bartender's outfit?

Kuru: Oh.

Mai: Shizuo.

TarouTanaka: Wait, you know Shizuo?

Kuru: Please pardon my brevity. Based on your chat messages alone, I would have taken you for a saint who could not kill a fly, Tarou, but you must have a wider social net than I realized if you know Shizuo as well. Perhaps if I were to meet you in person, you would turn out to be a great brute of a man, covered in tattoos and scars. Or a merchant of illicit pharmaceutical wares.

Saika: you mean shizuo heiwajima?

TarouTanaka: Sorry, there's so much to say about that, I can't even start.

TarouTanaka: Wait, you know him, too, Saika?

Saika: a bit

Saika: i'm sorry

TarouTanaka: Why are you apologizing? lol

Kuru: But sadly, it was not Shizuo whom we witnessed today. It was rather a playboy whose head was wrapped in bandages and an eyepatch. He was not a gentle fellow, but rather a finely muscled and sensual man.

Mai: He had a bunch of girls.

Mai: I was jealous.

TarouTanaka: Yes, very envious. And very impressive that he managed to stop a robber. He sounds like a policeman.
Kuru: Speaking of police, I just witnessed something interesting in town.
TarouTanaka: What was that?
Kuru: There were several dozen men congregated around a pedestrian bridge, shouting about something. They were completely packing the area.
Mai: Packed like sardines.
TarouTanaka: Ohhh.
Kuru: I believe they belonged to a motorcycle gang… Speaking of which, is everyone here aware of the Dollars? They're a wonderfully wicked and terrifying field of evil flora, a demonic darkness making its nest in Ikebukuro.
Mai: Dollars.
TarouTanaka: Umm, okay.
Saika: i don't really know
Kuru: Some say the name is short for "doleful callers," or "gang of people who are only worth a dollar," or "gang that will kill for a dollar," or the "devastating, overwhelming, ludicrous, lascivious, apathetic, raucous squad," but at any rate, the point is that they're a very mysterious gang! Despite being a classic color-based street gang, they rep no color at all in order to blend in with the city! It's an insane organization!
Mai: Really cool.
TarouTanaka: "Insane organization"? That's a bit much.
Kuru: But they are nothing if not insane. I mean, they're a group that has no discernable purpose or identity! If they were a typical street gang, they'd be taking out stress on the rest of the city, or doing it for money, or aligning themselves with a more formal yakuza operation—at least that would be fathomable. But the Dollars have no such thing.
Mai: No such what?
TarouTanaka: You're thinking way too hard about this.
Kuru: The Dollars have no fixed form. After all, how is one to identify a member of the group? Perhaps even ordinary students or housewives might be Dollars. Even a friendly classmate who comes up to say hello on the street might secretly be one of the Dollars… And we don't even know how many of them there are.

TarouTanaka: Well, yes, but…

TarouTanaka: But are you sure it's not just like any old club? There are plenty of places where anyone can claim to be part of it. It's like people who rep themselves as "Residents of Saitama," or "Metropolitans," or whatever.

Kuru: I believe you are misrepresenting the issue. The Dollars are not just a descriptor, but also a group; one must identify with the group in order to gain affiliation, and online or not, there is a type of community that they share. It may be a very loose network, but they are still gathered together under the Dollars' name. Don't you find that rather terrifying?

Mai: Scary.

TarouTanaka: Scary how, exactly?

Kuru: For example, it's as if there are security cameras all over the city, only the cameras are the eyes of the crowd. And unlike an objective camera, the observer paints the scene with their subjectivity. Also, the subject being observed has no idea that their actions are under observation. One wrong step out in public, and the Dollars' members watching you might detect and seize upon your most tender weakness.

Mai: Scary.

TarouTanaka: You're thinking too hard. It's not like that.

Kuru: …For now, I will choose to ignore the question of why you would so stridently take the side of the Dollars, a group no more important than a street gang. But how can you be so certain that the Dollars would never take advantage of unsuspecting people? They are a gang! Their very presence is antisocial in nature!

Mai: Gang up on the gang.

TarouTanaka: You've got a point.

Mai: Ouch.

Mai: I got pinched.

TarouTanaka: But while they might be a gang, I've heard it's more like a group that got together over a little joke on the Internet. Yeah, maybe they have IRL meetups every once in a while, but not to go on a rampage and terrorize people.

Kuru: I'll ask you again.

Kuru: How can you be sure of that?

Kuru: Let's say you are a member of the Dollars. Could you claim that no one else in the group has any ulterior motives just because you don't? There are many people in the Dollars, and I hear that no one knows who the others are... But if that were the case, don't you think someone could claim membership and use that to get away with something truly terrible?

TarouTanaka: Yes, you might have a point.

Saika: um

Saika: please don't fight

TarouTanaka: Uh, first, we're not fighting, lol.

Kuru: Of course not. I do not have a shred of personal hatred or anger toward TarouTanaka. The fact that we are members of the same chat room makes me like him enough to give him a kiss, in fact. Smooch!

Mai: Gross.

Mai: Ouch.

Mai: I got pinched again.

Saika: i'm sorry

TarouTanaka: Seriously, why do you keep apologizing?

TarouTanaka: Anyway, I understand that there's room to worry about that kind of stuff, but I haven't heard any bad rumors about the Dollars raising trouble in Ikebukuro, and even if they were, it wouldn't be any worse than the usual street fights that happen all the time.

Kuru: But that's not the case. Madness spins wildly through Ikebukuro, and the power of centrifugal force ensures that the lighter, inferior parts wind up at the outer edge of the rotation.

Mai: Spinny-spinny-spin.

Kuru: I understand that members of the Dollars have been picking fights with people from other prefectures. In fact, it was less picking fights than forcing them. Pounding their victims' faces to force the confrontation upon them, and whether they wanted to fight or not, they would beat and beat and beat and beat and beat their targets. It must have been quite a sight.

TarouTanaka: Huh?

Mai: I heard that, too.

Mai: That the Dollars beat up

Mai: some people in Saitama.

TarouTanaka: Is this true?

TarouTanaka: Do you have a source for that info?

Kuru: Are you familiar with the social media site "Pacry"?

TarouTanaka: I do have an account.

Kuru: What a fortuitous coincidence! Unlike with the site Mixi, one need only apply to register as a user. There is no need to receive an invite from a friend. Oh, pardon me—I did not mean that to sound as though you, TarouTanaka, have no friends. But I suppose that would depend upon your future actions. I cannot register, as I am below the required age for Mixi.

TarouTanaka: So where on Pacry is it?

Kuru: Oh! Please forgive me! I got carried away.

Kuru: If you do a community search for "Saitama Motorcycle Gang Problem," you will find a group based on that topic. I would look there first.

TarouTanaka: I'll do a search.

Kuru: One of the topics on that board should be titled "About the Dollars." That is where you will find the information I gleaned, but if it turns out that the account was falsified, then I will have confused you for nothing, I'm afraid.

Kuru: If that is the case, I will apologize most profusely and present my body and mind to you as payment… My body is a meager thing, its value questionable at best, but I would be honored if you found it to be a physical comfort to you.

Mai: Naughty.

TarouTanaka: Hang on, I'm checking now.

Kuru: You ignore me? Why, I am shrouded in desolation and loneliness. You must make things right by me.

Mai: Naughty.

Kuru: Someone claiming to be the Dollars started a fight with a motorcycle gang in Saitama. If this is an act orchestrated by some conspirator, then it was facilitated by the lack of a gang color. After all, anyone can represent the Dollars and frame the group for a crime!

Saika: that's scary

TarouTanaka: Sorry, I was just looking it up.

TarouTanaka: I've got some stuff to do after this, so I'll be leaving now.

Kuru: In that case, I suppose we shall take our leave as well.

Saika: good night

Mai: Good night, then.
TarouTanaka: Thank you.
TarouTanaka: Oh, and I'm sorry, Kuru. I think I might have upset you.
Kuru: Not at all. Do not let it trouble you.
TarouTanaka: Thank you. .
TarouTanaka: Anyway, that's all.
TarouTanaka: So long, everyone.

TarouTanaka has left the chat.

Kuru: Good night to you all. Golden Week is only just beginning, so please do be careful out there... I notice that Setton, Kanra, and Bacura are not here today.
Mai: Good-bye.

Kuru has left the chat.
Mai has left the chat.

Saika: good night
Saika: i'm sorry
Saika: i was too late

Saika has left the chat.

The chat room is currently empty.
The chat room is currently empty.
The chat room is currently empty.
.
.
.

Interlude or Prologue B, Vorona (Crow) and Slon (Elephant)

Russia

A comment mumbled in Russian traveled on the breeze to eventually settle upon the land.

"…Strange… This is not right."

A troubled man stood against the backdrop of endless fields.

He was not especially tall, but his figure was broad, and the thick, fleshy muscles that adorned his frame made him look larger than others his height.

The man was probably around forty years old. He wore a white coat over a white jacket, which gave him an appearance that a distant viewer might mistake for a polar bear. A number of scarves were wrapped around the top of his head and face, so that only a little gap was left, issuing periodic puffs of exhaust like a steam engine.

"Yep, not right. Oh dear, this could be trouble."

There were about ten other men around him. One of them, an older man with glasses and a grave expression, asked, "What is the matter, Comrade Lingerin?"

"Hmm? Oh…ohh. Listen to this, Drakon. It's all wrong."

"What is it?" Drakon asked, looking down at the first man's hands.

There were two round pots, with narrow openings. Lingerin had a hand stuck into the mouth of either one. "Look at this, Drakon."

"..."

Lingerin lifted his hands to show the other man. His looked somewhat like a boxer.

Drakon's calm expression never wavered. Without a drop of sweat, he asked, "What has happened, Comrade Lingerin?"

Lingerin waved his arms, his face deadly serious.

"My hands are stuck."

Silence churned through the group. Drakon merely lifted his glasses and set them down again.

"This is...quite a turn of events."

"I was trying to get the contents out, and then my hands got stuck. See?"

Anyone else would have scolded him for trying to tease or rolled their eyes at the bad joke, but Drakon gave him a perfectly serious answer—though it was given in resignation.

"Well, if it should come to it, you could always spend the rest of your life like that."

"No, I couldn't! How will I eat or use the toilet?"

"Nothing is impossible for Mother Russia. Throughout her vast lands there are surely those who would accept you warmly, Comrade, and give life to the seeds of a new generation."

"Hmm...? Have I just been killed off? Why do I feel as if you have skipped over quite a lot of time, Drakon?" Lingerin asked.

Drakon fixed his glasses again and said, "I shall make my point directly, then. Please give up on life—both physically and mentally."

"For being direct, that was certainly an indirect way to tell me to die. It's giving me the willies!"

"It was a joke, Comrade Lingerin," Drakon said without batting an eye, his features as placid as a wax figure. He decided to clarify his wishes.

"If you die, please wait until after we have overcome this challenge."

* * *

Lingerin turned to face the rest of the group. Unlike Drakon, their ages were impossible to gauge.

The men wore titanium helmets with bulletproof masks, assault armor, and vests with an assortment of pouches. Some of them even had gas masks on, giving the group the overall appearance of a special assault team.

But there was no consistency to their equipment, all of them using whatever gear they preferred. Some of them were carrying automatic firearms. Their presence brought an eerie tension to the Russian forest.

Lingerin surveyed the group and cracked his neck. "So what's the obstacle?" he asked.

"Thirty-seven armed illegals. It seems they were passing through the country to reach the west, and when we coincidentally became aware of their plan, they decided to come get rid of us."

"Coincidences can be scary. You sure it was a coincidence?"

"If you call it a coincidence that you bugged a car you thought was owned by a business rival, overheard their secret plan, admitted it, then tried to make a profit by selling them weapons—then, yes."

"You're right. It is a coincidence," Lingerin grunted, but the effect of his gruffness was lessened due to the pots stuck to his hands.

Drakon made no comment on his partner's appearance or attitude as he continued mechanically, "It seems they intend to raid the village we are staying in to steal all our product. Based on the speed and determination of their actions, I believe they might have been planning all along to steal weapons somewhere along the way."

"I see… So what you're saying is, they're like Thieves Without Borders."

"Not in the least, Comrade, but you are stupid enough that it will have to do."

"Good. Finding compromise is the mark of a valuable adviser, Drakon. I have full trust in you," said Lingerin Douglanikov, the president of a small arms-trading company—though it was hard to tell if the two were properly communicating their thoughts to each other or not. He cracked his neck and waited for the arrival of their enemy.

"What a pain in the ass, I tell you. If *they* were here, I could lie back in bed and enjoy my sleep."

"Are you speaking of our ex-employees Semyon and Denis? Or Comrade Egor, currently on leave?"

"No. Yes, they are all valuable men, but in this case, I am thinking more of certain specialists who will take care of such matters without even being asked," Lingerin said, like a child boasting about his favorite superheroes. Coming from a grown man around forty, he merely seemed drunk. As a matter of fact, he had already emptied his morning bottle of vodka.

"And they're the ones that Egor went on leave to find," the drunk muttered.

For the first time, emotion played on Drakon's features. "You mean Vorona and Slon." That emotion was faint disgust. "Yes, they are experts in dirty work. But compared to you, Comrade Lingerin, Slon is even more…well, you know…"

"More what? More…handsome?"

"I retract my statement. It is a closer race than I thought," Drakon said, his face placid once more. "As for Vorona, she possesses more beauty, grace, and knowledge than anyone else here…but at the same time, she is also more *enthralled* by a berserk need to fight."

He paused, removed his glasses, and grimaced. Lingerin smirked at his partner and taunted flippantly, as if there wasn't about to be a major battle, "Why, if I didn't know better, I'd think you were boasting about your *own daughter*, Drakon! If that was the point, why don't you call her by her real name rather than Crow?"

Drakon kept his expression hidden. He said to his employer, "I cut our family ties ages ago."

"And remember…they took our products with them when they ran off to Japan."

♂♀

May 3, Sunshine, Sixtieth Floor Street, Ikebukuro

Right around the time that a shoplifter began to charge through the milling crowds…

* * *

"Что случилось?" *(What happened?)*

The question belonged to a white man who stood out even more than the shoplifter in a way. There were plenty of black men around advertising for various businesses; foreigners were not a rare sight in Ikebukuro. But this man stood six feet tall, with limbs like massive logs and a professional wrestler's physique. With a sandbag-like sack slung over his shoulder, he looked just like a fighter preparing for a journey for training.

But the reason for the attention was the stunning contrast to the figure standing next to him.

"Нет проблем." *(No problem.)*

The reply came from a Russian woman, approximately twenty years old, carrying a large paper bag. Her features were young enough that *girl* might have been more appropriate than *woman*. But her figure was most certainly mature, and fine musculature was visible on her smooth, slender arms.

Her short hair was pale blond and dazzling, and little pupils stood out in the middle of her sky-blue eyes like deep pits.

The look on her face was cold, and there were scar-like marks here and there on her skin. In combination with her plain black clothes, she cast a dark aura on her surroundings. But that darkness only served as a pleasing, fascinating accent on the woman's finely chiseled features.

It was a veritable case of Beauty and the Beast.

Many in the crowd couldn't help but watch the pair until the ruckus caused by the shoplifter drew their attention away.

The girl showed no recognition of the reactions from the crowd as she turned to her partner and said flatly, "Denial, Slon… We speak Japanese in Japan. That was the decision. When in Rome, do as the Romans do. That is the basis of hiding one's body. I accidentally performed a Russian response. I will be more careful from now on. Both of us."

"I'm sorry, Vorona. It was my mistake."

"You stand out. We will enter our destination quickly. Please confirm."

Her accent and pronunciation were perfect, but her syntax and choice of vocabulary were off-putting.

The woman named Vorona and the man named Slon headed off to their destination. They had no interest whatsoever in the shoplifter and did not dedicate a second thought to the scene after that.

As the crowd around them eventually trickled away, a muttered comment hung in the air.

"A tepid country drowning in its own peace. Half disappointment. Half envy."

♂♀

A few minutes later, inside a karaoke box

"I can't. I can't do it. I'm too curious to take another step."

The pair entered a predesignated individual karaoke room, where they would wait for a certain contact to arrive—but as soon as they walked inside, the large man named Slon curled up and cradled his head in his hands.

Vorona, meanwhile, pulled a book out of her paper bag and began to read, flipping the pages rapidly. She said, "You are sitting. Deny your need to walk."

"I just can't help it… In the street back there, I saw a sukiyaki and a shabu-shabu restaurant. I just can't stop thinking about beef," Slon muttered, looking like the world was about to end. Vorona continued flipping the pages of the book without glancing at him.

"How…how do the cows grow so big when all they eat is grass?! It makes no sense that they can bulk up to that size from grass alone… I cannot undertake any jobs—I cannot even see a reason to *live* until I have solved this mystery!" he wailed, tears streaming out of his eyes.

Vorona continued turning the pages, but while her brain was totally fixated on the book, her mouth seemed to have a mind of its own. "A cow's stomach has special microorganisms, and the microorganisms react to the grass and saliva. They produce amino acids that the cow absorbs. Then, the cow grows. No problem."

"…"

She had accurately, succinctly answered Slon's question. Satisfied, his face shone with a brilliant light.

"Oh, I see! You're so smart, Vorona! Of course! Now I can eat steak with reassurance once again! It all makes sense now!"

But then…

"And I can drink milk! Of course, the picture of a human sucking on a cow's nipple is strange, but…but…oh… Now that I think about it…huh?"

A sudden thought caused Slon's head to sink down into his hands once again over the menu sitting on the table.

"I can't do it… I'm so curious I can't even look at the menu… Thinking about cow nipples made me wonder—why do men have nipples? What possible benefit do they have to procreating the species…? Damn! I won't move from this spot until I've solved the mystery of nipples! This is my war to fight!"

"There is a period in gestation when the fetus is neither male nor female. The sex is determined after the stage at which the nipples are generated. It is merely a leftover from that stage."

"Oh…ohhh… It's perfect! You're perfect, Vorona!" Slon exclaimed to the expressionless woman. "But…that brings a new question… and if I don't know this, I don't know how I can live in this world! Why—why are you not ashamed, Vorona?! When a man and a woman are alone and speaking suggestively of nipples and procreation?!"

Vorona replied to his idiotic question by flipping more pages.

She flipped.

And flipped.

And flipped.

And flipped.

And flipped, and flipped, and flipped, and—

"Are you ignoring me?!" Slon cried out at last, as Vorona finished reading her first book.

She pulled out a second and looked ready to say something at last, but the door to the karaoke room opened at that very moment, and a man appeared.

"Ahh, hello, hello, please pardon me."

An aging Japanese-looking man with a thoroughly friendly face looked through the doorway.

"Hello, hello, sorry about the wait. Hello," the man repeated, beaming as he took a seat. "I hope you'll forgive my haste, as I am a very busy man… I will get right to explaining your job."

He smiled all throughout his speech and pulled out two photographs to show the Russians without waiting for a response.

"The truth of the matter is…I need you to *abduct a child* for me."

"…"

The first photo was of a little girl with a doleful expression on her face. She couldn't have been more than elementary school age. Slon took the photo with his brow furrowed, while Vorona continued to flip the pages of her book, despite being in the midst of a negotiation.

The aging gentleman did not react. He continued his explanation.

"This is the granddaughter of the local yakuza boss—ah, yakuza being the Japanese mafia, ha-ha. I want you to kidnap her without killing her, if at all possible. Ha-ha-ha, I'm sorry about this. I know, you're usually hired killers rather than kidnappers. I know, I know."

"You might be the client who brought us to this country, but our participation will depend on the money. We can perform this job without being identified, but making an enemy of the yakuza carries its own considerable price," Slon said in quite fluent Japanese.

The man chuckled politely. "Well, you see, that is its own tricky problem. As it happens, they've hired their own bodyguard for the child. It is hard to imagine, but if the rumor is true, he is quite a dreadful fellow."

Bodyguard.

The mention of that word was the only thing that could stop Vorona from flipping pages.

"Protection is powerful? Confirm or deny. Quick answer is desired," she demanded.

The aging man smiled amiably at her and murmured, "Well, you see…it's not even a matter of strength or weakness… This one is almost like a magician."

"?"

"There was some footage on the Internet, so I downloaded it very hastily before coming here…"

The man had already produced a portable video player from his pocket and was playing a video on its small screen.

* * *

It was footage from a news program.

A group of what appeared to be criminals were on the run from a police car, as well as a mysterious figure on a black motorcycle swinging an enormous scythe at them.

"This is somewhat of an urban legend around these parts, known as the Black Rider… Who can say what sort of trick is being employed to create this effect? All I know is that if you try to mess with the girl in this photo, he will have something to say about it."

The man lowered his face in apparent consternation—but his expression still contained a smile. He looked sidelong at Vorona, whose face wore an emotion she had not yet expressed here.

"I have one question."

Vorona's cheeks were flushed, and her mouth curved upward into a delighted smile. She did not bother to hide her excitement.

"Will you allow me to kill this biker?"

The question was meaningless.

Slon did not consider himself to be a smart man, but he knew something about his partner.

Vorona was born with an innate berserk desire for battle.

With the carrot of fighting a mystery foe dangling in front of her, there was no way she would refuse this job.

He also knew another thing about her.

No matter how their client, Jinnai Yodogiri, answered her question, Vorona was going to attempt to kill this biker.

With these facts in mind, Slon calmly decided: *I don't get it, so I don't care.*

And so the mysterious Russians, their abilities still kept hidden, willingly stepped into the realm of the abnormal.

But then again, to them, the present situation of unrest and unease could be considered perfectly normal.

The Black Market Doctor Gets Sappy, Part Three

Don't worry. She's fast asleep.

Internal medicine's not my forte, but I had a feeling she had a case of acute pharyngitis.

Huh? Teething fever?

No, teething fever is something that only happens to babies, or toddlers at best. You know, just because we call it "knowledge fever" in Japanese doesn't mean it's caused by thinking too hard.

Then again, Shizuo, your brain is about equivalent to a toddler's, so maybe it would apply to you— *Bublagh!*

...

Listen, your forehead flick does about as much damage as a normal person ramming their knee into my face, so be a little more judicial in how you use that, all right? How long did that concussion knock me out?

I never thought I'd have to adjust my own jaw back into place. It's a good thing I have plenty of experience dislocating and relocating joints.

...Yeah, when my grandpa started choking on a mochi once, Dad dislocated his jaw so he could reach down and fish it out of his throat with his bare hand. That's a technique reserved for emergencies, though.

But enough about that. What's the deal with that girl? She didn't have any identification on her.

...What do you mean, "You better not have done anything weird to her"?

Listen, before you even start accusing me of being a lolicon, can you imagine me trying to put the moves on any girl other than Celty? If that was *Celty* moaning with fever on the bed, you can bet I'd be using my own body as a blanket to keep her warm!

And if Celty didn't exist, I'd probably be a hermit on some distant mountaintop, soaking in the majesty of nature. The only thing that can compare to Celty's breathtaking beauty is the entirety of the earth... That's my point. In fact, I still think Celty wins in that competition. What do you think?

...Hey, Shizuo, why does that guy Tom over there keep shooting me these pitying glances?

Why aren't you saying anything?

Well, whatever.

Huh? Celty?

Celty's out doing work for Mr. Shiki from the Awakusu-kai.

Yes, Shiki.

Their controlling operation, the Medei-gumi, is about to break bread with the Asuki-gumi, so it seems they're quite busy right now... He had some very important job to ask of Celty.

...

Yes, well, I'd be lying if I claimed I wasn't worried.

I mean, you know what kind of business the Awakusu-kai is involved in, right? A precious, gentle girl like Celty isn't suited to that world of bullets and blood... Actually, I'm kidding. I think she's perfectly suited to it.

A pitch-black rider weaving through a hail of bullets. Isn't that cool?

But I digress—I *am* worried. I wish she'd just stay with me at all hours of the day, but sadly, I'd only drag her down.

Still, I'm reassured by her strength.

Celty is strong. Mentally and physically.

In fact, Shizuo, it's kind of overlooked because you're monstrously powerful, but Celty is actually quite strong in her own right. She can take one of those metal pipes and twist it just like that, too.

She can take a hit from a car and keep going. It does still hurt her, though, from what I understand.

But she could be surrounded by ten or so of your average thugs and be perfectly fine. Now if it were thirty, she might get a bit scared.

She has certain weaknesses: a fear of certain types of supernatural topics and police bikers, but I think the presence of weaknesses makes her more lovable as a girl.

More than strong, she's cute. Isn't that nice? Isn't that great?

You can't have her, Shizuo. She gets along with you—and that makes me jealous.

...Huh? It's Tom, right? Why are you making that face?

Celty? Yes, that's right. I'm talking about the Black Rider.

She was a girl all along...? You never explained that to him, Shizuo?

...Huh? You didn't know that Celty was a girl until recently, either? I can't believe this!

Just look at her enticing center of gravity! Just a glimpse of her voluptuous outline beneath the shadow should be enough to entice physical desire, you cads!

Yes... If you don't need a head to love a person, then you also do not need a head to desire them. In fact, when I was in high school, I didn't feel a single ounce of desire for the normal girls. But Celty was different! When I was a kid, Celty was like a big sister I could count on, but now that I've grown to adulthood, she's more like an adorable kitten. Though in that case, I might be a rat.

...Sorry, that got a little sappy. But I don't regret it.

Let's get back to the girl.

What in the world did you do to get a little girl you've never met before to tell you to "drop dead," Shizuo?

I can see why you wouldn't know, though. You're the kind of guy who accumulates grudges without realizing it.

Let's say that one day, you pull out a tree lining the boulevard to use in a fight.

Let's say there was a girl who lost her mother years ago, and that very tree budded from the ground on the very day the mother died...

So when you pulled that tree out of the ground, you were tearing out the memento of her dear departed mum, and thus you earned her eternal ire... You never know.

That's just an example, though.

I certainly think it's more likely than the possibility that this sweet little girl is a wanton, indiscriminate killer.

Saika?

No, not that. Her eyes weren't red, for one thing.

But whatever the reason, it's a good reminder that people can be murderous toward one another for the smallest reasons. That's a fact, whether you can imagine that reason or not.

It just *happens* to you out of the blue.

Sometimes, misunderstandings and misguided revenge are involved.

However, even at the point you realize you're angry because someone is trying to kill you over a misunderstanding...doesn't change the fact that they're trying to kill you. You just have to overcome that situation.

Besides, maybe it's not a mistake.

Trivial things that you did in the past can turn the lives of others insane. It happens all the time.

And then, there are people who do those "trivial things" on purpose.

Like Izaya.

Ooh, that got a real nasty look on your face.

Why can't you two just kiss and make up already?

...Or wait, were you *ever* on good terms?

Ahh, that takes me back. High school!

For being our green, inexperienced youth, it sure was red all the time.

It was always blood, blood, blood around you and Izaya.

But thanks to you, I got a lot better at setting bones and sewing stitches, ha-ha.

I don't hate Izaya, as a matter of fact.

He's just very honest about his desires. The same way you're honest about your emotions.

In Izaya's case, it would have been so much easier if the target of his desires were straightforward, like money or women.

Instead, he had to get involved with "human observation," whatever that is.

Watching other people and feeling superior to them is such an infuriating hobby, don't you think? It just makes him arrogant.

He was clever enough to be aware of his situation, so he didn't rub too many people the wrong way—but he would use his findings to say the one thing that will shock and unnerve a person the most, without drawing their hostility.

...That Tom fellow seems to want to say something. What is it?

...You think I'm observing people and basking in my own superiority more than anyone else? Oh, geez. Looks like *I* was the one who rubs people the wrong way after all.

Well, as long as Celty still loves me, I don't really care.

Gosh, I wish the three of us could hang out again, just like we did back at Raira Academy.

Standing back at a safe distance while watching you and Izaya try to kill each other was, like, my daily routine.

Speaking of which, I wonder how it is for the students at Raira now.

Um, well, I don't really know them, but at the big hot-pot party, Celty knew a boy there named Mikado Ryuugamine. Oh, and I know the girl named Anri Sonohara. You met her once when you were here with a gunshot wound, remember? Also...do you know Seiji Yagiri and Mika Harima? You were there at the party, right?

Huh? You know Seiji?

He stabbed with you a pen? What?

Well, anyway... For the most part, they seemed pretty well-behaved.

Mikado and Anri are like perfectly ordinary modern kids who would never get into a fight.

They seem to be sharing some kind of secret with Celty, but the thing about secrets is, with little kids and girls, they can be alluring. The mysterious beauty. The mystery children. It's nice, like a movie subtitle. A big sweaty guy with a secret is just a suspicious creep up to no good.

...Why did you look at me when I said the word *creep*?

Well, anyway…

I wonder how youth is for kids growing up nowadays.

Back when we were in high school, you and Izaya pretty much ruined it for me, except that I was happy because I had Celty to go home to each and every day.

It's a nice thing, having a home to return to.

It is a bit worrisome that they seem to know Izaya, though.

Youth is a writhing thing.

It squirms and wriggles in the mud.

Youth is considered to be the "springtime" of one's life… But spring is not always some fanciful fairy-tale time.

It's also the season when all the bugs and squirming things that people hate come crawling out of the earth.

Perhaps that youth might turn out to be one of the worms or grubs in that swarm.

They all hope that they don't turn out that way, but as I said earlier, you never know when you might be earning the hatred of someone else.

In Mikado's case, just being an acquaintance of Izaya means he's treading in very dangerous waters.

And of course, meeting *you* at the hot-pot party means they're now officially treading into a hellish hot pot of troub— *Blrrgfh!*

Chapter 3

THE DAYS OF YOUTH SHINE AND CRUMBLE

Russia

"So, where were we?"

Lingerin's hands rattled as he shook them, still stuck inside the pots.

But in contrast to his jaunty tone of voice, the place where he stood was one of raw violence.

The stench of blood filled the room. But even stronger was the pungent smell of gunpowder, the haze of smoke blotting out the red accents that covered the floor here and there.

A pile of bodies lay around Lingerin's feet. Men of obviously foreign origin, presumably the illegal stowaways mentioned earlier, now sacks of flesh, their heads and torsos streaming blood.

And yet the men still living were virtually unchanged from before.

Drakon stood at Lingerin's side, wiping steam residue from his glasses, while the men in special-forces gear warily eyed the surroundings in silence.

"We were talking about Vorona and Slon, Comrade Lingerin."

"Oh, right, right. These guys came and interrupted us. They were not aware of the situation. That's how you wind up dead," Lingerin murmured heavily. He spread his potted hands wide and exclaimed, "Awareness is a very important skill! Denis and Simon were always very good at that. Certainly enough to scamper away to Japan just before we faced our greatest test."

"You mean the time that we raided the security company hired by our business rival to send them a message."

"*Hoo boy*, I sure thought I was going to die then. Well, that was a case where I was not being very aware. I failed to anticipate that they would have a whole boatload of former Spetsnaz in there. We were missing on purpose to threaten them, but they were very inconsiderate and actually tried to kill us!"

Drakon studiously placed his glasses back on his nose as his employer guffawed and stated clinically, "When the military was heavily reduced postperestroika, many Spetsnaz lost their jobs. As a means of employment, many wound up in private security and the mafia—a warning which I have given to you approximately twenty-three times since the dissolution of the CCCP, but it seems you were not listening."

"How was I to know? Most of the members I knew went straight into mercenary work… Besides, is this really the time to criticize me? Surprisingly you seem to not be attentive, Drakon."

"The most potent lack of awareness in this scene is the state of your hands, Comrade Lingerin."

It was not said with hatred, disgust, or anger. It was simply the truth: His employer looked like a bear that had gotten both paws stuck in beehives.

Lingerin slowly turned away and then laughed to draw attention away. "It's not as if I did this on purpo—"

A pot burst with a sudden eruption of noise.

Emerging from the right-hand pot was the gleaming barrel of a pistol. Smoke trailed upward from the muzzle as shards of broken pottery rained down onto the bodies on the floor.

A second later came the gurgling sound of spilling liquid.

Drakon looked down to see that a foreign migrant lying on the floor, who had *previously been playing dead*, was now drooling blood from his mouth. The gun he'd pointed at Lingerin fell to the floor.

"…I suppose I must offer you my compliments," Drakon sighed.

Lingerin burst into a delighted beam. "Of course… I should I have shot my way out! It's a shame about the pot, but it was cheaper than this gun…I think!"

"I am more curious about why you needed to put the gun in the pot in the first place. And why didn't you just let go of it to remove your hand? And on top of that, if they were fragile enough to give way to a bullet, why did you not just smash them against the wall?"

"I have no idea what you are saying. Speak Russian, man."

"Did the words that just came from my mouth sound like English or Japanese? Very well. If this is an issue with Wernicke's area, the speech center of the brain, then the anomaly must reside in one of our brains. Let us visit the hospital together. I look forward to learning which of the two of us must be sent to the sanitarium."

Drakon's words emerged as a hunk of freezing dry ice. Lingerin's eyes bulged, and he shook his head to dispel the illusion before returning to the topic at hand.

"As I was saying—Vorona. She might be twenty years old, but she's still a child inside. She's very good at her job, but the drawback is that unlike Semyon and Denis, she is not aware of things."

"But this is a matter greater than awareness. They violated our most sacred of unspoken rules. If I have the opportunity, I will crush their skulls and spill their brains myself."

"Very scary. And who says that about his own daughter? I'm willing to say that I'm not angry anymore. You can go easy on her by merely locking her in storage, can't you?"

"The warehouse? I would think that starvation is a much more painful end than gunshot," Drakon said, straight-faced.

Lingerin cackled and ran his tongue over his lips with delight. "So you're saying an execution is unavoidable? Listen, we're not military or mafia. Let's play it loose, my friend. All this talk about killing—it makes you sound a bit barbaric, don't you think?" Lingerin noted, sitting in a room full of grisly corpses. "For one thing, you don't even have the skill to kill Vorona by shooting her."

"Affirmative. I am ashamed to admit that I cannot stop her. Is that not why we sent Egor to Japan? If need be, he can enlist help from Denis and Semyon. But…from what I hear, Egor already suffered a major injury fighting against one of the locals."

"Japan is scary in its own right, eh? Our illustrious president is adept in the ways of the Japanese art of judo—perhaps it was a judo master he ran into? Oh, right, I should break the other pot."

Lingerin pointed the gun in his right hand at the pot covering his left. Drakon put a hand on his shoulder without looking and said, "I will not quibble with your choices anymore, but I believe that breaking it with the grip would be better than shooting your own hand. As for Japan, it is a very vexing situation. If she learns that Egor was taken unawares by a local, Vorona will most certainly not take it lying down."

"Now, now. Your daughter is very human in nature, compared to you, you robot. She acts on her instincts and desires and does not hesitate to kill. And she'll kill for reasons other than food or defense, so it's a very human instinct, not like other animals."

He struck the butt of the gun against the pot, breaking it apart. Inside, his hand was holding a piece of honeyed beef jerky, which he lifted to his mouth and started to chew. "But for a human, she's definitely one of the crazy ones."

"As ironic as it is to say this in your presence, Comrade Lingerin, Vorona is still immature as a person. It is the result of leaving my young daughter alone to be raised by books after the death of her mother. She has much knowledge, but her mentality is still that of a child," Drakon lamented, half blaming himself for the outcome.

Lingerin waved his hand breezily. "Oh, it's all fine. She's in the midst of her youth, eh? You've got to get out there and mix it up while you're young. The spring is warmer in Japan than here, right? Let her enjoy it."

"The only problem is, she stole a couple of very grown-up toys from our stock before she left."

♂♀

May 3, on the road, Ikebukuro

The woman in the riding suit—Vorona—calmly accelerated her motorcycle as she glanced at the distant figure splayed on the ground.

"..."

Meanwhile, something rustled past, a fine glint that slipped around a loop of her belt.

No one could have possibly noticed the tiny glimmer of light, as the sight of the collapsed motorcycle and rider occupied all the pedestrians in the vicinity.

Meanwhile, the cars behind the scene had no choice but to either stop where they were or turn down side streets to avoid the mess.

Vorona rode down a cross street herself, feigning being yet another spectator. Once she had confirmed in her mirrors that people were beginning to gather and murmur at the scene behind her, she took off into the night without a second glance.

She knew why they were buzzing over the scene. She herself had seen it happen.

It was the sight of the Black Rider's helmet flying high into the air and the headless body slamming into the ground.

"..."

Under her helmet, Vorona was silent with thought as she sped through the night streets. Eventually, she arrived at her destination.

A lonely, quiet street occupied by a single truck.

The truck was her own, an undercover vehicle with the logo of a fictional company on it. Slon was on standby in the driver's seat, and as she approached, he flicked the hazard lights on briefly.

Vorona pivoted the bike over to the rear of the truck. As she did so, the back doors swung open, and a metal ramp automatically extended down to the ground. She rode the bike right up and into the cargo hold of the truck.

Half of the space was like a little warehouse, with plenty of other material stored away in addition to a platform to carry the motorcycle. The front half of the hold was built like an RV, with a white fur sofa and a closet.

Vorona stood in front of the closet and forcefully removed her helmet and riding suit. She wore nothing but a thin T-shirt and leggings underneath, her well-balanced body shining in the light.

There was internal electricity, just like in a real RV, with an outlet near the living space in addition to the lights. She had taken off her T-shirt, leaving only a bra on underneath, when Slon's voice came through the wireless receiver on the table.

"Nice work," he drawled from the driver's seat up front. *"Are you changing now?"*

"I affirm."

"It's too bad I can't see that."

"It is not too bad for me," she replied. She slipped briskly into a fresh T-shirt, neither ashamed nor angry.

Taken aback by that brief answer, Slon changed the subject. *"By the way, while I was waiting I saw a car pass by with the license plate one-three-one-three, and it made me wonder… Why is thirteen considered an unlucky number? I feel like I'm dying to know the answer. Is that the curse of thirteen?"*

"Many theories exist. Most famous is thirteenth seat at the Last Supper, seat of Judas. But not all are rooted in Christianity. Legend of Norse gods. Twelve gods provide harmony. Harmony broken by appearance of Loki, the thirteenth. In ancient times, cultures used duodecimal systems. Thirteen breaks the harmony of twelve. Hated number. Too bad."

"I see—not that it makes me feel much better. Say…are you sure we can't speak in Russian? I can speak Japanese to a degree because it was pounded into me years ago…but your Japanese is kind of stiff. It's weird. It'll give people the wrong idea and make them dislike you."

"Denial. Topic of work will be understood, no problem. I will be hated. No problem," Vorona replied.

From up ahead, Slon said, *"I don't really get it, but if it's no problem to you, then that's fine."* He wasn't going to rack his brains worrying about it. He started driving the truck.

Meanwhile, Vorona had finished changing into her normal clothes and sat down on the couch. "That was too simple. Disappointment. Black Rider is too weak."

"You say something?"

"No relation to Slon."

"None of my business? Never mind, then," he quipped.

Vorona waited for him to stop talking and then closed her eyes and let her mind work.

I am disappointed.

I thought a monstrous person like the one in the video would satisfy me.

But he was utterly careless. Nothing short of a mindless thug.

How could he fail to notice the special wire looped around his neck, connected to the traffic light?

I thirst.

...I thirst.

♂♀

If youth was meant to signify the "spring of one's life," then despite the fact that she was twenty this year, she had not yet reached that point.

Vorona had never loved another human being.

Not even herself.

She knew that the emotion called love existed. But she was unable to determine if it was necessary in her life—for she had never experienced it outside of knowing it as an abstract concept.

As a child, she grew up by watching her father's back.

But it was not because she idolized him.

Her father, code-named Drakon, had never attempted to see eye to eye with her. He gave her books to pass the time but always kept his back to her, focusing on any direction other than the one in which she existed.

"That's just love. He's turnin' his back to you to protect you from the rest of the world, miss. Drakon's just a clumsy, stubborn man, so he'll never let it show, that's all," said Lingerin, the man her father worked for.

She did not understand what he meant because she didn't know the meaning of love. She was merely bewildered.

But she never felt lonely.

Her father kept plenty of books around the house, and she had the right to read any of them whenever she wanted.

If she asked for a book, he would buy it for her without question or comment.

Lingerin was amused by the way she could read at many times the normal speed and would gather up strange books from foreign countries to give to her as gifts.

Surrounded by paper, she absorbed everything she could get her hands on into her brain, from knowledge necessary to survive to utterly useless trivia.

Her father did not love her, and she could not love anyone else. But she was not particularly unhappy about her plight.

She didn't associate much with the other children at school, and they had been warned to stay away from her by their parents, who knew that her father was involved in a dangerous business. So she lived a solitary childhood.

Even still, as long as she had books, she was happy.

She had never felt the thirst—until the moment arrived.

The very first time she felt the thirst was when she committed her first murder.

The night that a burglar broke into the house and she killed him using knowledge she gained from a book.

Largely through coincidence and good luck, she made use of a method that she knew to kill a man.

She was just a little girl, just barely ten years old, who could hardly shoot a gun all alone.

The human body stopped moving much easier than she imagined from reading the books.

When she witnessed this phenomenon for herself, an eerie breeze blew into her mind.

It was several years later that she recognized the feeling that swirled through her mind was thirst.

When her father got word and raced home to see the motionless corpse of the burglar, he silently embraced his daughter.

He hugged her blankly, like a robot, but she could still remember the warmth of his arms.

The young girl thought.

I don't understand, but Father is facing me.

He is making a connection with me.

Why?

What did I do?

Is it because I beat a bad man?

Because I killed someone stronger than me?

Because I *was strong?*

They were very silly, childish conjectures.

And even in her childish state, she could sense that it was undoubtedly *something else.*

But she was not able to understand love. And thus she could not have possibly understood exactly why her father hugged her.

Instead, she clung to a different premise. Or more accurately, pretended to cling.

After that, she began to learn things she couldn't find in books from Denis and Semyon, her father's subordinates.

Denis and Semyon were on the younger side within the group, but it wasn't known what they'd done in the past. Lingerin, the company president, did not seem preoccupied with such details, and from what she could tell, Denis had been in the military, but that was it.

Just that little bit of information was enough for her. She asked the two of them for information on various weapons and ways to fight. Denis claimed that it wasn't the kind of stuff to teach to kids, and the only things Semyon would teach her were about her own physical discipline.

But once she began helping out with her father's business, they started to teach her how to use weapons, bit by bit. It was just a minimal amount, only enough for self-protection—but she turned those lessons into means to defeat others.

It started with hoodlums in town.

Next, the drug dealers with their weapons.

Next, a low-level mafia with battle experience.

Next, two of them, at the same time.

Next, three.

Then, four, five, six.

She raised the stakes with each successive attempt, and every fight she survived brought her the satisfying sensation of her own power.

One day, when she came across a rival group to her father's company and learned that they were planning a raid, she approached the group by herself—and defeated them.

When Lingerin got word and visited the scene with his men, all he found was the air full of the smell of blood and gunpowder, and a little girl, totally unharmed, reading a gossip tabloid she found in her targets' office.

This time, her father did not give her the warmth of an embrace, but a stinging slap across the face.

In that instant, she realized something—she was not shocked in the least that she had been slapped.

In fact, she understood, deep within her, that it was a justified action.

For years and years.

From the very moment she killed that first burglar.

And with that understanding came another truth.

If she knew that her father would not praise her, why had she done this thing?

Why did she continue to wage war against so many other people?

She hadn't done it for the want of love.

It was simpler than that.

It was fun.

It was enjoyable.

It was thrilling.

It was pleasing.

It was deranging.

In short, she had been telling herself a cheap, transparent lie: that she wanted her father to pay attention to her. When all along, what she was really doing was indulging in her own pleasures.

Ironically, it was a worried slap from her father that made her realize this, but afterward, whichever direction he faced was no longer her concern.

With the stops removed, she rapidly grew more powerful and also steadily crumbled apart.

Lingerin likened her to a crow—very smart, yet choosing to scavenge the dead—and jovially gave her the nickname "Vorona," along with an official position in his company.

Through Lingerin's jobs, she continued to eliminate countless "enemies."

But her thirst was never quenched.

Because her father never hugged her again, like that very first time?

No.

She already understood that was not the reason.

Was it because she was a bloodthirsty killer?

Technically, that was not the reason, either.

She did not really like defeating people.

She did not like killing people.

She just liked punching hard things and feeling them crumble.

Breaking through multiple layers of defense, cutting apart finely disciplined muscle with a knife.

Cracking through the fine seams in modern heavy armor—sometimes inserting gas, sometimes bullets—and shredding apart the fine, soft flesh inside the shell.

Confirmation.

All she wanted was to confirm.

It was a kind of desire for knowledge, perhaps.

Fragile. To her, humans were so terribly, terribly fragile.

But was that really true?

The first burglar she killed was far more fragile than she'd imagined, based on the books.

And so she thirsted.

Killing a person as a child had left a scar on her heart.

And just as some people cannot stand to let a wound go untouched, she could not go without picking at that scab on her heart.

Was it truly a human being she killed back then?

Are humans really so fragile?

Was she just as fragile as the others?

No matter how rigidly trained, no matter how heavily armed, no matter how experienced in battle—was a human being nothing more than a water balloon of flesh, hanging on bones as hard as quartz?

For whatever reason, she grew uneasy if she was not constantly seeking that confirmation.

She did not know why.

She just continued seeking out new foes...

And so she ended up working on her own, as a freelance jack-of-all-trades, in the biggest city of a country devoid of battlefields—but not by her own intention.

♂♀

"Okay! As you just heard, I am everyone's favorite idol, Eiji Takemo, and it's time for today's broadcast of *Lightning Russian Paradise*! My partner, as always, is this sweet bilingual baby speaking Russian and Japanese..."

"Я рад встретить всех вас сегодня! That means, 'I'm happy to meet all of you today!' It's Kieri Murata! And why are you starting off with 'baby' right at the drop of a hat?"

"Whoa, whoa, what did you just say? 'At the drop of a hat' isn't something a proper Russian would say! Kieri, you've got to eliminate that Edo Japan from your speech and work on exuding a proper Russian sexiness! You know, the way they do up north in the snow! Where you take off that heavy fur coat to reveal nothing but lingerie!"

"Замолчи Трилоби́ты!"

"Huh?! Wait! What did you just say?! You just said something in Russian!"

Vorona's eyes opened slowly to the sound of a raucous radio program.

Half sleeping.

Slon must have turned on the radio up front. She looked at the clock to find that hardly any time had passed at all.

Through the wireless, she heard a familiar braying laugh drown out the radio.

"Ha-ha-ha-ha-ha-ha-ha! Did you hear that, Vorona?! 'Shut up, trilobite,' she said! Even we don't use the word trilobite *as an insult! Ha-ha-ha-ha-ha-ha!"*

"Affirmative. But it is not worth laughing as much as you have. Also, I am slightly stunned by your knowledge to understand and translate 'Трилоби́ты' to Japanese."

"Your dad taught me very thoroughly. He read tons and tons of Japanese newspapers and novels to me."

"I escaped. Bond of family is cut. The next time of meeting, one of us will die. Too bad, so sad." That shifted the conversation abruptly from mundane to deadly. But Vorona's face was as devoid of expression as ever. "I have murdered the bodyguard riding the black motorcycle."

"That's good news."

"When the child's location is found, word will come. Until then, there is need to complete different job."

"Right... You did accept another job, didn't you? Do you really want to do it, though? I thought it wasn't your style," Slon asked.

Vorona pulled a book down off the shelf and flipped it open to where she had marked it. "There is no problem. We will act within the night."

She picked up the photograph she had used as a bookmark.

This is the target.

It's true. I don't like this.

Hurting a normal girl, one with no training of any kind. I will feel guilty about it, and more importantly, it will be very boring.

Perhaps the client is putting the blame in the wrong place...but I cannot help it. It is my job.

Vorona resigned herself to the job and looked down at the photo again, committing its features to memory.

A girl with round glasses and reserved features.

Anri Sonohara.

The name written on the background sheet given to Vorona did not inspire any particular reaction.

It was only recently that she arrived in this city. And she had no particular interest in the neighborhood known as Ikebukuro.

Of course, even within Ikebukuro, there were very, very few who understood the true nature of the girl named Anri Sonohara.

But at this point in time, Vorona hadn't the slightest clue what it meant to join that exclusive circle.

I am very disappointed by the Black Rider.

...On the other hand, I didn't think he was going fast enough to knock his head off...

But what's dead is dead.

Humans are weak, even the magicians.

She had only seen a brief snippet of footage from Yodogiri.

Which meant that she did not know.

She did not know what the Black Rider, Celty Sturluson, was called in breathless excitement by the national media of Japan.

The Headless Rider.

No matter how hard she tried, she couldn't sever a head that was never atop Celty's shoulders to begin with.

But that information could not be found in any book she had ever read before.

That was why she didn't know.

She couldn't be wary of things that were beyond the bounds of common sense.

If she was going to go to those lengths, she might as well be clutching good luck charms as she carried out her jobs, hoping for protection against the vengeful ghosts of her targets.

Celty Sturluson happened to be that far outside the bounds of what she knew.

Furthermore, Vorona never once noticed the abnormality of her own motorcycle.

Tangled around the rear of her vehicle was a very fine line about the width of a hair.

The pitch-black thread continued outside of the truck and off somewhere into the night.

And she certainly did not know the very unnatural source of that string was currently in hot pursuit.

♂♀

May 3, night, Internet café, Ikebukuro

"And now…"

The voice was very upbeat and pleasant.

At the risk of sounding corny, anyone who heard that voice might say, "It was like the blue sky above was speaking to me." That was how crystal clear and harmonious it was.

"Things should be getting interesting," the voice's owner said, looking at the text on the screen of the cell phone.

A handsome young man, looking very pleased with himself, was lounging in the middle of the Internet café.

At first glance, he might seem mild mannered, but his features were on the bold side, a perfect manifestation of the term *suave*. In contrast with his all-accepting smile, his eyes held a disdain for everything that was not himself. His overall look, fashion and all, was unique, yet no single feature stood out—an odd man whose nature was impossible to grasp.

Despite the fact that Izaya Orihara was sitting in front of a computer connected to the Internet using the café's facilities, he ignored it and fiddled with his phone instead.

He absorbed the information flowing out of the little world nestled in the palm of his hand, filing it away inside his head, and muttered, "That takes me back to the high school days."

He was giving a monologue, speaking his innermost thoughts aloud, but no one was there to respond.

The seats around him belonged to young people lacking a residence who rented those spots as a home for months at a time, but they were out working night jobs at this hour.

Izaya negotiated with the café proprietor to rent out his seat for a *year*. Whatever bargain he had struck with the business owner was apparently allowed as a special individual case.

He organized the information he'd just learned into a summary of the present situation and got to his feet.

It really does take me back.

Then again, my youth was a royal mess, thanks to Shizu.

If it weren't for him, I would have done things so much better.

In fact, I think I must have spent half my effort in high school just trying to crush him.

Izaya waved to the front desk as he made his way out of the place. He chose not to take the elevator, savoring each and every step of the staircase as he descended toward the night street.

As the ground-level exit approached, a warm gust of spring air and the unique bustle of a shopping area enveloped Izaya's body. He let the air permeate him and could not prevent a smile from twisting his lips.

I just can't help it. Even imagining the scene makes me smile.

No matter how events play out…

Only I will be able to slip through the mosquito net.

* * *

One month earlier...

Izaya Orihara had been completely out of the loop for an incident that occurred in Ikebukuro.

He'd be lying if he claimed that this didn't frustrate him.

He felt as if other people had left him behind.

Izaya Orihara loved people.

He did not love any individual person in particular.

He himself was human, and he loved the very thing we call "humanity."

That might be considered a very grand form of self-love, but in his case, he did not count himself among the humanity that he loved.

No, more precisely, he was in love with "other people."

That moment had been the perfect opportunity for him to observe the creatures he loved so much, but he missed it. During that incident when an enormous bounty had been place on Celty's shoulders, he was left in the dust.

Calling this payback made it sound so petty.

It would be petty—but an undeniable part of the reasoning behind his actions.

He started this in the same way that a petty man would kick over a bicycle out of frustration at being left out of the fun—but the trouble with Izaya Orihara was that he was *fully* cognizant of that part of himself.

He was absolutely, objectively aware of his personal situation and emotions and continually chose the worst possible options for those people he loved so much.

Izaya Orihara was not an abnormal being like Celty or an invincible warrior like Shizuo Heiwajima. He was a perfectly ordinary human.

He was not even the calm and mechanical type, the sort who could kill without emotion.

He was a regular person through and through.

It was simply that he simultaneously possessed both the greed of a normal human being and the will to violate taboos if they stood in his way.

He was not some charismatic mad villain; he just lived true to his interests.

Back in high school, Shinra Kishitani told Izaya, "You know, you tend toward the evil side, but you're not totally evil. But you don't have a shred of goodness, either. If I had to sum you up in one word, it would be—*sickening*. I mean that as a compliment, though."

Izaya snorted with derision at his friend's comment, but he knew it to be totally accurate.

He forced his targets to be sick, spitting up their true natures, and he calmly observed from a distance safe from the splatter.

He just observed human nature.

Whether it was lofty ideals or contemptible bile that was spat up, Izaya loved and treasured all the answers equally.

They were all facets of the humanity he loved so much.

And today, he began a new game intended to expose the nature of people.

The players were assembled. The board was open.

He just had to roll the dice.

"Time to give those sweet, sweet kids at Raira a little present."

"Just the right level of danger to promote a healthy level of personal growth."

Izaya Orihara thought to himself…

It's fine being out of the loop.

The people sleeping inside of the tent can't kill the mosquito flying outside of it.

All I have to do is buzz my noisy little wings as loud as I can.

Over and over, without stopping, until the people inside slowly, inescapably go mad.

"A proper youth needs some thrills to spice it up."

Izaya fiddled with his phone as he walked.

Shizuo Heiwajima, Simon, and his own two little troublemaker sisters.

He had numerous foes in Ikebukuro.

But he strode freely through the neighborhood's streets—blending in with the city, silently, so silently.

The mosquito outside the tent began to ring his poison quietly into the night.

And for his first chirp, Izaya set off the ringtone of a particular young man.

After a few seconds, a timid boy's voice came through the phone.

"Nice to talk to you again, Ryuugamine. Or should I call you Tarou-Tanaka?" Izaya teased. He switched into a more serious tone to say, "I just checked the backlog of the chat room. I've heard a bit about this Saitama incident."

"...Sounds like there's some real odd business going on with the Dollars."

♂♀

May 3, night, Anri Sonohara's apartment

The interior of Anri Sonohara's apartment was truly simple; in fact, it was unbelievably tidy for the residence of a teenage girl.

It was typical for a serious, dedicated student to have a clean apartment, but in her case, this transcended clean into the realm of minimalism.

There was nothing to be found outside of living necessities. She didn't even have any books or magazines to read for fun.

A TV and a radio also adorned the room, almost by obligation, while school textbooks were stacked on the room's desk.

The interior was certainly lived in, but it was impossible to gauge the nature of the apartment's resident just by looking at it.

Anri Sonohara was the sort of person who lived in such an apartment.

There wasn't even a computer in the room, but she did have a cell phone, and she stared at the screen in silence, dressed in her pajamas.

It displayed a chat room that she logged into from time to time. The chat was managed by a woman(?) nicknamed Kanra, but Setton was the one who invited Anri there. No one had actually stated that Kanra was a woman, but as Anri was largely ignorant in the ways of the Internet and human communication, she did not know that there were men who pretended to be women online.

Celty wasn't in the chat today. It was…nerve-racking…

Anri thought about the headless knight that went by the username Setton in chat and let out a long sigh.

Were there others in the chat who knew that Setton was Celty?

The question rose to her mind but did not lead to any further thoughts.

It was fun just watching the chat. But without Celty, her only actual acquaintance in real life, she felt more tension than usual being in there today.

Anri had been joining in at a Net café originally, but Celty recently taught her how to access the chat room on her cell phone, so she was doing her best with fumbling fingers to type in messages with the keypad.

As she didn't have many friends, the chat room was a rare opportunity for her to communicate with others. It was a contact different from what she experienced at school, and she hesitantly, steadily dipped her toe into this new world.

Still, it was frightening to be there without the nickname Setton in the user list.

Realizing once again that she was a terribly weak person, Anri closed the Internet window and placed her phone in the charging cradle.

It was time to sleep. She reached out for the chain on her overhead light.

Just then, the doorbell rang, eerie in the night apartment.

She felt a nasty shiver run down her back.

It was eleven o'clock at night. Most people might not find the ringing of the bell to be eerie. But Anri did not know of any friends who would come by to ring it at this time of night.

Despite the eeriness, Anri couldn't just ignore it, either. She headed over to peep through the hole.

She glanced around, but there was no one in sight.

"…?"

And then she did something she should *not* have done.

Under the assumption that she was safe with the chain on, she unlocked the door.

The instant she peered through the gap, an enormous pair of shears thrust itself into the doorway and clamped hard on the chain.

By the time the loud snap of metal echoed off the walls, it was already too late.

The door burst open to reveal…a woman.

Huh?

She wasn't able to process it in the moment.

All she saw through her glasses was the figure of the woman.

The instant she saw the body shape under the tight clothing, she recognized that it was female. But the facial features were invisible to her.

The woman was wearing a ski mask with goggles over the eyes, completely hiding her head from view.

"Eeeh—" Anri started to scream—but the woman pressed the pruning shears around her throat before the cry could escape.

"Quiet. I will not kill you. You are relieved," came a statement from the ski mask in perfectly accented Japanese that was nonetheless rather strange. "You will be immobilized for some days. Possibility of several months. But there is no need for death," the emotionless woman said.

"Huh…?"

"I will avoid vital area. I will call an ambulance."

"Umm…"

"You are very blissful."

And with that, the woman drew back the hands holding the pruning shears—and plunged them directly toward Anri's soft belly.

♂♀

A few seconds earlier, driver's seat of the truck

Honestly, if they needed some normal girl roughed up, they couldn't have asked any local ruffian? Why did they need us to do this? wondered Slon as he sat in the driver's seat of the truck, looking at the picture of their target.

Of course, you never know if some local idiot would get carried away and kill her, and if a man did it, there's always the possibility for danger of a different kind... Maybe having Vorona do this was the right call after all.

He sat back in his seat with the engine idling and his thoughts equally idle, when...

He heard something odd mixed in with the sound of the engine.

"...? Thought I just heard something."

At first, he was ready to dismiss the distant noise as irrelevant.

But he found that he couldn't ignore it. The sound he'd just heard was the kind of thing he knew he shouldn't hear right smack in the middle of Tokyo.

That sound...

Slon's eardrums throbbed again with the same vibration.

I knew it.

Certain that he hadn't misheard it now only made the question loom larger.

Why is there a horse whinnying in the middle of the city?

It was the fierce, eerie sound of a horse crying out.

Was there a racetrack or a stable around somewhere? He decided that had to be the answer, but it was still an odd thing to hear in such an urban environment.

If this were New York, he could assume that it was a police horse. But he'd never heard of such a thing being used in Ikebukuro, Tokyo.

And for another thing, this particular whinny was creepier and more "emotional" than any Slon had heard before.

What is it? Is that really a horse?

Just as his curiosity started turning into unease, he realized another unsettling fact.

The sound was steadily approaching.

...?

Sweat began to bloom on his back. Alarms blared inside his head.

Normally, it might be the sort of problem he could safely ignore. But his vast experience working for Lingerin the arms dealer gave him keen instincts, and those instincts were screaming *danger.* It was the same feeling he had when Lingerin pissed off that private security firm run by ex-Spetsnaz.

What is it…? What's coming this way?

Slon held his breath, glancing nervously into the rearview mirror.

And he saw…

A motorcycle even blacker than the black of night.

And sitting atop it, an abnormal figure holding an enormous scythe.

♂♀

Meanwhile, Anri's apartment

The whinnying of the horse approached.

Vorona felt something alien in that sound, but any thought she might have devoted to it was absorbed in a different sound altogether.

Metal.

She should have thrust the shears into the side of the girl's torso at a proper angle, enough to cause a hospitalizing injury. But the feeling that reached her wrists was not that of supple young flesh being pierced.

It was an unpleasant rigidity, as though the shears had bitten down on a metal pipe.

"…Что?" she mumbled accidentally in Russian.

She looked down at the girl's torso to see that the shears were halted just in front of their target by another piece of metal.

Японский меч? (A katana?)

It was a long, smooth blade.

The gentle backward curve of the metal was like the surface of a pristine water droplet.

What…is this?

The girl was secretly holding a katana, and she brought it forth to intercept the attack—an unlikely conclusion, perhaps, but certainly possible.

Yet there was an even eerier phenomenon in Vorona's view.

"Um…I'm sorry," mumbled the target, who was *growing the blade* directly out of her arm.

"I don't know you. Are you sure you don't have the wrong person…?"

♂♀

Anri Sonohara was a normal human being.

Up until five years ago.

Of the many fates of those who associated with the "abnormal" such as Celty Sturluson, hers was to house the abnormal within herself.

When Shinra's father, Shingen Kishitani, cut the dullahan's soul to sever the head from the body, he used a cursed katana to do it. And "cursed" was the only way to describe this particular weapon.

Shingen sold the blade, known as Saika, to an antiques trading shop run by Anri's father. Through a series of events, her parents then died, and she wound up bearing the cursed blade within her own flesh and blood.

It wasn't the sword's fault that her parents died. If anything, without it, she and her mother would have died at her father's hands.

It was a painful thing to accept that either way her mother would have died anyway, but Anri chose to accept the cursed blade as the price to continue her own life.

Anri thought how much easier things would be if only this cursed blade was like the ones in the old period tales, where the curse completely took over its victim's mind.

Or how much more delightful it would be if, like in comic books, it would become a conversation partner that she could have a fun chat with whenever she wanted.

But the curse of Saika, the one she actually had to deal with, was much nastier in nature.

Saika had only one desire.

To love people.

To love all humanity.

That was it.

But to Saika, "love" meant being one with the other. To be one with all humanity.

She would sink her curse into all human beings on earth, filling them with her words of love, filling the world with "daughters" that shared her consciousness.

That was the entirety of the Saika system, Saika's curse.

But Anri could momentarily hold back that curse. By viewing the world around her as though through the frame of a painting, she could reduce even the overwhelming, maddening words of Saika's love to nothing more than a distant landscape.

At the moment when she felt her mother's love and her father's lack of it, Anri's mother was cutting her own belly open with Saika. And thus Anri felt an enormous unease and a certain kind of kinship toward Saika and her desire to love humanity—as well as overwhelming envy.

Just look... See how much Saika is able to love something. She seems so blissful.

When she realized that was how she felt about it, Anri felt terribly guilty, though not toward anyone in particular.

Saika, meanwhile, would not save Anri from her plight.

Since she could not cut the host that gave her life, Saika determined that Anri was not a target for her "love." Anri idolized Saika, and Saika used Anri, even as it was trapped within her. It was not quite symbiosis, but a kind of circular parasitism.

If there was one thing that Saika could offer back to Anri—

It was the many "experiences" that were chiseled into Saika's consciousness.

♂♀

The moment that the shears touched her body, Anri realized that she had already twisted herself to put distance between her and the woman.

The memory of all that battle in Saika's mind flowed into Anri's body. She unconsciously made use of it, using her delicate figure in the most efficient manner possible.

"I don't know you. Are you sure you don't have the wrong person...?" she asked, her brain hastily pushing everything through to the other side of the painting frame.

She saw what was happening as though it were a distant scene. Not that you needed to be in Anri's shoes to lose a sense of reality when a strange woman with her face covered up attacks you with a pair of pruning shears.

Praying that it really was just a misunderstanding, and determined to handle things as quietly as possible, Anri consciously moved the blade growing out of the rip in her pajamas over toward the palm of her hand.

Like the tail fin of a shark crossing a sea of white skin, the tip of the katana slid down Anri's arm until it reached her hand, where it burst forth. When the full glory of Saika was at last revealed, it fit neatly into her palm.

"Um...if you're hoping to rob me...I have no money. Please leave," she begged.

Vorona clamped her mouth shut and gave the girl an instantaneous examination. She found that the target's eyes glowed a faint red.

As though the entire eyeball itself shone with red light.

John Carpenter's remake of the movie *Village of the Damned* was known in Japan by the title *Glowing Eyes*. That little piece of trivia she read just days ago throbbed in her brain—not that it was any help in understanding the situation she now faced.

What is this? Vorona wondered, her brain full of question marks. *What is this girl?*

But her body still moved automatically. She twisted, plunging deeper into the sword's range, and swiveled her elbow upward toward the target's jaw.

But just as suddenly—

A shiver ran through her entire body.

A thought flickered into her brain: *Oh, I'm going to die.*

Vorona canceled her elbow attack and leaped backward. At almost the same moment, a flash of silver passed right before her nose.

Based on the location and speed, the slash was probably not meant to kill. It was a slice intended to hurt, not to cleave.

And what would happen...if I was cut?

She understood that the blade before her had appeared in a way that should have been impossible. Combined with the overall eeriness of its appearance, it was right to assume that even *touching* the sword meant great danger.

What is this girl? Is she...human?

She was an unknown—something that did not match Vorona's knowledge or experience.

Coming face-to-face with such a thing brought about a complex emotional response within her.

...I feel...hot. I remember this. I felt this...before...

The sensation arising within her was very close to the sensation that she felt the first time she killed a person—right at the moment before she took his life. Vorona distanced herself farther from her target.

I have lost my calm, she recognized and tried to force her mind to cool down.

But just then, she heard the raucous horn of the truck.

—?!

She looked over to see that their vehicle, parked at the side of the apartment building, was flickering its lights madly to get her attention.

Emergency situation.

Vorona's mind was ice-cold once again. She looked back at her target and announced, "You, mysterious. Very strange."

"..."

"I will appear again. Happy to see you then."

She ran off for the truck, careful to keep an eye on the girl so that she didn't get sliced down the back. The target did not seem to be giving chase, but before Vorona could feel any relief at that, a new abnormality hit her ears.

The whinnying of a horse.

The bellow was coming from extremely close to the rear of the truck, and it floored Vorona with its eeriness. Still, she did not let it shake her too much and gave a curt command to drive as she passed by the driver's side of the truck.

Tires tore against asphalt, hurtling the massive vehicle forward. As Vorona leaped onto the back of the truck, she saw the abnormality approaching—and realized that it was not an abnormality, but a monstrosity.

A pitch-black motorcycle without a headlight was slowly approaching. Not racing. Just pacing, measuring, confirming.

It was the very rider whom Vorona had decapitated minutes earlier. She recognized it at once.

Not because of the sleek black motorcycle…but because the person riding on it had no head above the shoulders.

…?

It was more confusion than fear.

Due to the rapid succession of bizarre events, she had to wonder if she'd been slipped a hallucinogen somewhere along the way. It could have been a dream—except that everything about it was too *real* for that.

In either case, it is dangerous.

The situation was too extreme for inaction to be an option, "just in case" it was a dream.

Vorona deftly opened the rear door of the truck as she clung to the back bumper.

—?

She noticed something odd.

She hadn't noticed it before, but there was something like a fine thread running through the seam in the door and into the interior of the truck. It continued to the rear of her motorcycle.

The moment that bike became visible through the open truck door, the whinnying roared, fiercer than before, and the pursuing bike sped up.

That sound…it's coming from the bike!

With this realization came another new fact about the black motorcycle.

Before, she hadn't noticed because the exhaust of her own bike would have drowned it out anyway—but aside from the whinnying, the black motorcycle was not making any engine noise whatsoever.

Danger!

The street outside Anri Sonohara's apartment was particularly sparse by Ikebukuro standards. There were hardly any cars or pedestrians to be seen.

But that would only hold true until the next light. After that, it was urban Tokyo as usual, the traffic network where cars ruled above all.

Even if the truck used its weight to muscle the other vehicles around, the motorcycle would catch up to them in less than a few hundred feet.

Danger! Danger! Danger! Danger!

Vorona's decision was bold in the extreme, and the transition to action lightning fast.

She rolled into the cargo hold, ripping the cover off an object that was placed close to the door.

The Black Rider sped up all the while, closing in on the rear of the truck. But when the rider saw what appeared from under the cover, the bike instantly slowed.

The object was a gleaming mass of metal formed into a threatening shape: an anti-matériel rifle using fifty-caliber rounds.

It was a gun designed to attack tanks and helicopters, and if the right ammunition was used, it could pierce the hull of an armored tank from up to a mile away.

She had brought the rifle in the unlikely chance that they needed to escape police cars or choppers—but she certainly hadn't foreseen using it in a situation like this.

Vorona got down on her right knee, lifted the gun, and placed the stock against her right shoulder. It weighed over twenty pounds, but she brought it into firing position with practiced ease.

It should be noted that using a fifty-caliber round on a human target is forbidden by international law. Vorona knew that fact because she had read it somewhere or other, and she remembered Lingerin saying, *"You can't shoot people with this because it blows them apart like red water balloons. It's a bitch to clean up."*

But Vorona could not identify a motorcycle rider without a head as "human."

Still, she did not aim it directly at the rider's torso, either because she had her own misgivings or because the motorcycle itself was an easier target.

In either case, Vorona set the sights on the body of the motorcycle, as she had done to an armored car once in the past, and pulled the trigger without a second thought.

Eruption.

Ikebukuro rumbled with the sound of a cannon, and the pedestrians walking around outside instantly covered their ears, unable to pinpoint the source of the noise.

A few seconds later, lights turned on in the apartments nearby, and windows opened as residents peered outside to see what the commotion was about.

Vorona, meanwhile, was unable to see the result of her gunfire. The smoke from the anti-matériel rifle completely engulfed her.

The wind from the truck's acceleration whipped the smoke clear momentarily, but for those few seconds, she was effectively blind—and when the smoke was gone, the Black Rider was gone.

Neither was there the wreckage of the bike.

Thanks to the unique make of the gun, the kick was not as bad as the force of the shot would suggest, but given the circumstances, she was not in the mood to continue firing it for now. She set the gun down to examine the surroundings better.

When it became clear that the black thread was still connected to the rear of her own motorcycle in the cargo hold, she took out her shears to cut the tiny sinew. But it was far tougher than she imagined, and she had no luck severing it.

"Slon. What has happened to Black Rider?"

"I don't know. I don't know if it's gone for sure, but it's not in the rear-view mirror. Did you actually use that thing, Vorona?"

"Affirmative. It was an emergency."

The truck eventually came to a stop—they must have arrived at a light connecting to a major street.

Vorona hastily shut the rear doors right as the light turned green, and the vehicle turned into the thoroughfare.

After a few seconds of thought, Vorona touched the black thread and traced it back to her bike, where it was tangled all around the rear of the vehicle. She took the wireless receiver and ordered, "There should be a scrapyard nearby. Head there, please."

"What are you going to do?"

"My motorcycle was being traced. We will scrap it," she muttered without emotion, a trait she learned from her father. She thought for a few more seconds.

"Or perhaps we might set a trap and lie in wait."

♂♀

Outside Anri's apartment

"Celty…!"

When she heard the eruption of noise, Anri raced out the door without thinking.

She was still confused over the attack she'd just suffered, but even more surprising was the sight of a truck driving away with her attacker clinging to the rear bumper and the familiar monstrosity chasing after it.

A few seconds later came an eruption that sounded like a cannon going off. Anri ran out into the street, so worried about Celty that she was oblivious to her own danger.

"Watch out," spelled a message on a PDA screen flying in front of her face. A hand reached out from the side and pulled her back toward the apartment.

Anri turned in surprise and saw the riding suit without a head atop it. "Celty! Wh…what?"

She'd just seen Celty riding off after the truck. Why was she standing here?

Celty shrugged and typed up a new message: *"Well…it seemed like…I was going to get shot… So I put up a really thick shadow shield to block it, and it pushed me all the way back here. Or…blasted me, I guess… Yeah…that was kinda close…I guess. Shooter could have been…pulverized."*

Celty's insertion of all those ellipses was probably a sign that she was still trying to process what happened.

Right behind her was the bike, and in Celty's hands was a horribly distorted hunk of metal. That had to be what was left of the bullet.

"I was going to chase after them, but they clearly don't mind firing guns in a residential area. If we get them too worked up, who knows what'll happen to the people around here..."

"Guns...? You mean..."

"Why were they after you, Anri?"

"Actually...I have no idea," she mumbled, looking troubled. "Do you think they'll come back?"

Celty pounded her own chest reassuringly. *"Don't worry. You should stay at our apartment tonight. The security's good there."*

"B-but..." Anri hesitated. Celty waved her hand back and forth in front of the space where her face should have been.

"Don't hold back now. You've stayed there before! It's already too big as it is—and we can think of a plan to deal with them!" Celty said, and Anri had no reason to refuse anymore.

"Th-thank...you...," she mumbled, accepting the headless woman's offer.

Celty, meanwhile, raised a hand to her own shoulder in consternation and typed, *"By the way, do you have a mask or helmet or anything?"*

"Huh?"

"I accidentally left my helmet out in the road...and when I went back to get it, a dump truck had squashed it flat where it lay... I'll have to go back home to get my spare," she explained desperately.

Anri thought it over. "Um...can you do what you did for me before and just make black helmets out of your shadow...?"

Silence fell between the two momentarily.

After ten seconds, Celty turned away shyly, forming a rounded shadow helmet, and held out her PDA.

"Right, I forgot..."

♂♀

Thus, the first day of Golden Week came to a close.

Each and every being involved bore their own abnormalities, without realizing the troubles that others had fallen into.

* * *

The night passed, giving way to the morning.
The sunlight was exactly the same as on any ordinary day…
And the sun gazed down upon the disaster unfolding in Ikebukuro.

♂♀

May 4, morning, Mikado's apartment

Didn't get much sleep after all…

He slumped into the desk chair in front of his computer, covering his exhausted face in his hands.

After hearing about the Dollars' rampage in Saitama in the chat last night, Mikado had gone on a furious fact-finding hunt.

It wasn't his duty, and no one else forced him to do it—but he couldn't escape the feeling that he just had to do this.

As one of their founders, Mikado felt as though the Dollars were like a part of his own body.

They weren't necessary for him to live. But just like cell phones and the Internet, once you made it a part of your ordinary life, it was very hard to cut loose. Such was the importance of the Dollars to Mikado.

On top of that, the Dollars were not booming in number the way they once did, but it felt like the group was still growing. Even Mikado did not have an idea of their precise number at this point.

And because of that, he was always fearful of the gang going out of control. He had even shut down the Dollars' home page for a time.

When the circle of friends had just started the page, they created a joke rule that "all new members of the Dollars must confess the worst thing they've ever done" and then set up a registration page on the site.

That page no longer existed for two reasons.

One, the comment field to publicly confess those deeds wound up being used as a kind of chat forum and, at its worst state, contained links to pirated downloads and cracks for computer games found through other forums. It stopped following its intended function.

Two, the "confession of evil deeds," which was created as a joke, steadily turned into something that was very much *not* a laughing matter.

At first, the entries were all about stealing snacks or drawing eyebrows on dogs, but the content slowly escalated until words like *shoplifting* and *assault* started showing up.

Then, people started looking down on others for the tepid nature of their confessions, trying to play up their bad side by bragging about their exploits. By the time they were writing things like "I shoplifted for the first time ever so that I could join the Dollars," Mikado decided to shut it down.

The Dollars were created to be fun. They weren't meant to destroy the world, or lower the level of morality in society, or play at being outlaws.

So if this rampage could be stopped, he had to do it.

He had no idea if that was possible or not, but he would be shirking his duty as one of the founders if he didn't at least try to find out.

At least, that was what he thought.

Until he got a call from Izaya Orihara several hours ago.

♂♀

"Hello, Ryuugamine speaking."

"...Nice to talk to you again, Ryuugamine. Or should I call you TarouTanaka?"

"We haven't talked on the phone in forever, Kanra."

"I just checked the backlog of the chat room. I've heard a bit about this Saitama incident... Sounds like there's some real odd business going on with the Dollars."

"...Yes, I was just looking into that myself."

"How much did you figure out?"

"I'm pretty sure that it's new members of the Dollars doing this independently from the rest of us."

"Yes, I figured as much. So what's your plan?"

"Well, I want to stop them, but..."

"Why?"

"Uh..."

"Was there ever a rule in the Dollars that you can't go into another prefecture to start a fight? What reason is there to go reining them in now?"

"But..."

"Or did that brouhaha with the Yellow Scarves make you wise up with the whole 'playing street gangs' thing? I've heard that it caused a terrible rift between you and a close friend."

"That's not true. Masaomi's still my friend."

"Let's hope he feels the same way."

"...Why are you stirring things up like this?"

"Oh, trust me, I'm just jealous of my alma mater juniors, thriving in the throes of their youth. I didn't have friends like that, you see. I only had one pervert that kept sticking around and one hateful, violent cretin."

"..."

"Anyway, back on topic."

"Yes?"

"Whether you like it or not, the Dollars you created already have real form and power. There are going to be people who want to pull down others in order to sell the reputation of the gang...and thus raise their own reputation as well. It's inevitable."

"...I understand that."

"It's fine. The Dollars' lateral connections are very weak, so even if the people from Saitama look for revenge against the ones who attacked them, all you have to do is stay quiet and let it blow over. Isn't that how the Dollars work? You save the people you care about and sit back and be lazy toward those you don't like. You have freedom. You're free to do what you want."

"...You called me just to say that?"

"Er, no, no. That's not it. But the Saitama thing reminded me. You guys got attacked by those motorcycle gangs last month, right?"

"Um, yeah. We made it through all right, thanks to Celty and Kadota..."

"One of those gangs at the time was the one the Dollars just attacked in Saitama."

"Uh..."

"Their leader has a terrible weakness for women... And *he's the kind of guy who will resort to violence in a snap. He kicks people down onto the ground, then jumps feetfirst onto their faces."*

"Wow, he sounds dangerous..."

"Very. So I wouldn't go walking around at night with girls, understand? Like your friend Anri—I'd be very careful with her."

"...Sonohara has nothing to do with any of this."

"Does she? What if someone finds out that you're a member of the

Dollars and that there's a girl you have feelings for...? There's no guarantee that this hypothetical person is the sort that wouldn't *bring innocent people into this. They're here for revenge, remember?"*

"..."

"Besides, you've used the Dollars plenty of times already. Remember the squabble with Yagiri Pharmaceuticals? Do you really think you have the right to say, 'Don't do bad stuff,' now?"

"...What should I do, then?"

"How about you think for yourself, rather than asking others for the answer?"

"What I think is that I want to do something. It's what I've been telling you all along."

"Ha-ha-ha. So I can't coax you that easily. At any rate, if you don't want Anri to be involved, and you yourself don't want to get dragged in, then you should forget about the Dollars. Push them from your mind. If only until the heat dies down, you know?"

"But..."

"Let's say that you really do want to stop the Dollars from beefing with other groups... Or you want to stop the Dollars from just randomly attacking other people... Even if you could achieve such a thing, it wouldn't be the Dollars anymore. If your singular will could control the actions of the entire group, it would be something else entirely...but you don't need me to tell you that, do you?"

"No, I understand that."

"I happen to think that the Dollars fall under a much broader definition than just a color-based street gang. Maybe they're not a country or a culture...but there are people with many different ways of thinking within the group. Some are good, some are bad. But you don't know what people outside of the group will think of you. Will they see the good Dollars or the bad Dollars? That's not a choice you get to make."

"..."

"Sorry, I've been doing all the talking, haven't I? Am I annoying you?"

"Er, no. Um...thanks. For everything."

"..."

"...Is something wrong?"

"Mikado."

"Yes?"

"Are you a bit excited?"

"…Pardon?"

"Oh, I was just trying to imagine what sort of face you're making into the phone right now."

"What kind of nonsense are you talking about?"

"Well, this is that 'extraordinary' you love so much, isn't it?"

"That doesn't mean I'll like *anything*, as long as it's not ordinary."

"Are you sure?"

"Of course I'm sure…"

"When you temporarily closed the Dollars' site, you claimed it was because the registration page was being trolled and the confession of evil deeds was escalating out of control… I can buy the former, but I'm not so sure about the latter. Was it because you found them to be in poor taste?"

"Well, obviously."

"If you really thought that way, you wouldn't try to maintain the Dollars at all. You'd try to erase them and pretend they never existed. Or you'd just quietly slip away and be a normal person again. All you have to do to leave is ignore the e-mails. There's no punishment."

"I'm one of the founders… I can't be that irresponsible about it."

"Yes, you can. Nobody in the Dollars expects you to take responsibility. And if you still insist on doing so, that would mean you're extremely conscientious… But you're not actually that kind of person, are you?"

"What is this all about?"

"You know what? Never mind. You'd rather not know what other people think of you, would you?"

"You can't just bring it up and then drop it halfway… Tell me. I'm not going to obsess over it."

"You won't? Well, this is only my personal conjecture, so don't take it personally if I'm wrong. It's just an info broker joking around."

"Got it."

"…It's not the Dollars going out of control that you're afraid of, is it?"

"Uh…"

"Aren't you just afraid that they're going to change and leave you behind?"

"That's not true!"

"..."

"Ah..."

"You were very quick to deny that. You should be careful about hasty denial; it only increases suspicion. Or maybe you already recognize that about yourself?"

"..."

"You're not a big fighter, and you're not some trashy punk. I bet you've never smoked or drank in your life, and you're disgusted at people who brag about committing theft. You're a normal, productive citizen. That's a very honorable thing, but I bet you felt bored with that honor and created and maintained the Dollars as a response to it. An escape from your ordinary life. Wasn't that your dream?"

"..."

"See, I'm worried about you."

"Wha...?"

"What did I tell you before? In order to enjoy your everyday life, it has to always be evolving. And it's not the kind of thing you can bottle up, then just keep inside yourself."

"Kanra... Mr. Orihara..."

"Just Izaya is fine. Kida calls me Izaya, too. You shouldn't forget that even outside the Dollars, you have many people on your side. Not just Anri and Kida...but me, too, if you ever need the help. So you shouldn't worry yourself sick over what's happening now, all on your own. That's all I wanted to tell you."

"Um...Izaya."

"What?"

"Thank...thank you."

"I haven't done anything to deserve your thanks."

"You never know. I might be manipulating you into doing some plot of my own... Just kidding."

♂♀

Mikado remembered the conversation and smiled wryly to himself.

I always thought Izaya was a mysterious, fishy weirdo who was always up to something.

But it turns out—he's just a nice guy.

It was that easy for Izaya's words to cheer Mikado up. If he hadn't been so agitated about what was happening with the Dollars, he might have remembered what his best friend said on the day he first came to Ikebukuro.

"Don't ever mess with Izaya Orihara."

In a way, it was a crucially important warning. But that did not register in Mikado's brain today.

Because Mikado still did not know the full breadth of what Izaya did to Masaomi.

After that, the boy focused again on devising a plan. Except…

"…I can't come up with anything…"

He really was grateful for what Izaya said at the end, but he couldn't deny that he'd also suffered a bit of a shock from their conversation.

He had no idea what he really wanted.

Do I…actually want to stop the Dollars from going out of control?

He didn't actually know who had done what in Saitama yet. But it was undeniable that some kind of violence had happened there under the Dollars' banner.

But I definitely don't feel excited about this, he told himself. Yet deep down, he wasn't sure that was true.

Yes, he wished to escape his ordinary situation more than anyone when he started the Dollars. That was essentially still true today.

Despite the fact that he met the greatest possible example of the extraordinary—Celty Sturluson—Mikado could sense that something was smoldering deep within him.

…I'm a coward. Just like Izaya says… I've never had a real fistfight with anyone, and I've never been beaten by a group of people.

It was presumptuous of him in the extreme to assume that he could control the entirety of the Dollars.

That feeling of uncertainty bloomed within him, and time passed without any change. Now there was sunlight shining bright through the window, and the hands on the clock said that it was nearly nine o'clock.

"…I don't have any time left for sleep."

He was supposed to meet with Anri and Aoba at eleven. There wasn't much he needed to do in preparation, but if he started snoozing now, he'd probably sleep right through their meeting.

Fortunately, he'd napped yesterday evening after getting home from school. He was just pulling a nutrient drink from the refrigerator, assuming that he'd be able to manage, when—

The doorbell rang.

"?"

Who could that be?

Probably just a newspaper subscription salesman. They'd come by several times before, and Mikado always made up an excuse through the door to send them away. They typically left without another word, probably assuming that the run-down apartment didn't house people with much extra cash to spare anyway.

But that didn't mean he didn't have money. In fact, Mikado raised all of his living funds aside from school tuition on his own. When his parents were against him moving to Tokyo, he convinced them by claiming he would work to pay for everything aside from tuition. Even then, his parents still sent him a bit of spending money here and there—but he gratefully deposited it into savings.

While his work was technically part-time, the variety of Net-based businesses that he worked with required a lot of time and trouble in total, so it was a significant drain on his schedule. Being able to pull that off and support himself while keeping up with his schoolwork was actually quite a feat, but Mikado didn't consider himself particularly special. It was just what he needed to do on a regular basis.

He accepted the doorbell as another part of his ordinary circumstances and opened the door without thinking.

The bright morning world burned his late-night eyes, stinging the backs of his sockets. Mikado lifted a hand to shade his face from the sun as he looked out the door.

Standing there was the boy he'd met just yesterday and was scheduled to meet again in only a few hours.

"Good morning, sir!"

"A...Aoba?"

It was Aoba Kuronuma, the underclassman at school whom he promised to take on a tour around Ikebukuro today.

"What's up? We're not supposed to meet for another two hours."

Huh? Something tickled at the back of Mikado's head. *Did I ever tell Aoba where I live?*

"Well, actually, I needed to ask you about something before we met up with Ms. Anri..."

"You could have just called," Mikado said kindly. "And, uh, who told you my—?"

"It's about the Dollars," Aoba interrupted, smiling.

A nasty chill crawled across Mikado's spine. His face froze. Aoba leaned in closer, beaming angelically.

"It's a little awkward to just stand around here, so shall we go somewhere else?"

At that point, Mikado realized something was wrong.

Someone was holding the door open. Not Aoba, who was standing in the entryway, and not himself, of course.

A mystery set of fingers was holding the edge of the faded door, visible against the sunlight.

Aoba filled the silence with an eerie suggestion.

"It's okay if you need time to change. *The group can wait.*"

♂♀

Twenty minutes later, abandoned factory, Ikebukuro

In a district at a slight distance from Ikebukuro, where the streets were much lonelier than the shopping area, there was a spot among a line of factories that was particularly vacant.

It was the site of what had once most likely been an ironworks. The gray metal walls were stained with rust in spots, the sign of several years' passage since the property had been abandoned. There were piles of reddened scrap metal here and there, the machinery that would have processed them entirely dismantled.

For some reason, there was a nearly new motorcycle left in the factory, but its presence was less of an off-putting anomaly than a counterpoint that accented the rusted scenery.

It was a truly desolate locale, empty despite the clutter.

The inside of the dilapidated building rang with the excited chatter of youth.

"Whoa, what's with the ride?" Aoba wondered. "This wasn't here yesterday."

A hefty youth standing next to him muttered, "Maybe someone's hiding a stolen vehicle?"

The other boy was about as tall as Shizuo. He had tanned skin and tight muscles, the skin of his arms and neck that was visible under the tank top ribboned with tribal tattoos.

He wore a mustache over his menacing features—and certainly didn't look like a student—but Aoba introduced him to Mikado as a "classmate from middle school."

There were a large number of people surrounding Mikado now, in fact, and they jeered raucously at Aoba.

"Gross, there's gonna be roaches and centipedes all over this place. Let's go find some luxury hotel to use as our hangout spot."

"You gonna pay for it?"

"Shut up and eat your roaches."

"You eat roaches?!"

"Hee-hee!"

"How much will you pay me to do it?" "Three hundred yen." "That's it?!" "I'm in!" "Really?!"

"All right, let's go find a cockroach! Get some oil to fry it up!" "You won't eat it raw?"

"*Euurgh!*" "Don't puke!" "But…I just imagined eating a cockroach…"

"Hey, Aoba, can I sock the shit outta these obnoxious clowns?" "Nope." "Hee-hee!"

They had to be about the same age as Mikado. The assortment of youths in all stripes and shapes crowded around him, walking him toward the back of the factory. But other members of the group, present earlier but now absent, were clearly over twenty years old. They had driven the group to this place in their cars.

Why did I follow them here?

None of it made any sense. It was obvious that he shouldn't have gone along with it, but it didn't seem possible to refuse or run away.

At the same time, Mikado felt something eerie about this particular factory.

Wait...I recognize this place, he realized with a start. *Oh! I was here...a few months ago...*

But before he could travel any further down that line of thought, Aoba seated himself on a nearby pile of metal and looked up at Mikado.

"Last night, you were asking around on the Dollars' member website about the fight that happened with the people from Saitama, right?"

The fact that Aoba was the only one smiling in his incessantly pleasant way was creeping Mikado out.

If Mikado had rather youthful looks, Aoba was practically a baby face. He didn't look anything like a high school–age teen, and yet here he was, smiling innocently in the midst of a group of hardened ruffians. Mikado couldn't help but get goose bumps.

"Y-yeah, I was. I had some concerns..."

"I know what happened. I wanted to explain it to you."

"Really?!"

For a moment, Mikado forgot the eeriness of the situation, and life returned to his features. Ordinarily, the suggestion that he "knew what happened," delivered in these circumstances, meant only one thing. But Mikado completely failed to anticipate that inevitability.

To Mikado, Aoba Kuronuma's appearance, attitude, and position were about the furthest thing from that possibility. So even when it was stated aloud, he was initially unable to understand what the boy was saying.

"That was us."

"...Huh?"

"We did that," Aoba admitted, never breaking his smile. "Me and everyone else here... We attacked the people in Saitama, *as members of the Dollars.*"

"...Huh? What?" Mikado's lips formed a vacant smile. He wanted to take it for a joke.

But Aoba's childish, innocent expression delivered only the truth.

"Look, you know that gang called Toramaru. The people who were chasing Mr. Kadota's van and the Black Rider last month."

"Uh, what? Ah, r-right."

"We burned a couple of their bikes and hospitalized a good twenty or so of them."

The menacing tattooed youth added, "To be accurate, you threw Molotovs right into the parking lot where they hung out, Aoba."

Only when the statement came from someone who actually looked like they could do such things did Mikado finally put everything together.

"...Wha...? But..."

But his sense of reason refused to accept it. He could only flap his lips uselessly and stare at Aoba.

Aoba went on, watching Mikado's eyes closely, soaking in the older boy's reaction.

"We *are* in the Dollars...but we've also got another name."

"...Another...name?"

"Have you ever heard of the Blue Squares?"

May 4, morning, chat room

Bacura has entered the chat.

Bacura: Good morning.
Bacura: Yeah!
Bacura: Wait,
Bacura: Nobody's here.
Bacura: That figures, it's morning.
Bacura: Well,
Bacura: It's been about,
Bacura: A week since the last time I was here.
Bacura: Really sorry that I haven't been able to pop in and chat more often.
Bacura: I was working,
Bacura: And hanging out all the way up in Tohoku on a love rendezvous with my girl.
Bacura: How's everyone been?
Bacura: Guess I'll go look at the backlog to see what everyone's doing during their vacation time. Yeaaah!
Bacura: Huh,
Bacura: Looks like the log prior to yesterday is just gone.
Bacura: Was there some sort of technical trouble?
Bacura: Anyway,
Bacura: See ya later.

Bacura has left the chat.

The chat room is currently empty.
The chat room is currently empty.
The chat room is currently empty.
.
.
.

Interlude or Prologue C, Aoba Kuronuma

Three years ago, apartment building rooftop, Ikebukuro suburbs

"...The hell do you want? I got my own shit to do, you know?"

The irritated young man glared down at the even younger boy.

The scenery visible from the rooftop was corroded red with sunset, and the man was shielding his eyes from the sunlight coming from behind the boy. The boy's expression was hidden in shadow, but the hint of a smile could be made out around his mouth.

The young man, Ran Izumii, did not like his little brother, Aoba Izumii.

When he saw the way his brother could be obliging and considerate of others, he couldn't help but feel an odd sense of irritation inside.

His brother hadn't done anything to him, and he wasn't held to be inferior to his brother, but it just seemed like the younger boy was the only one who ever received the affection of those around them.

Parental love, teachers' marks, even childhood friends—in every respect, his younger brother grew up with more love than he did.

He didn't particularly desire such a thing now, but he couldn't avoid feeling irritated whenever he was reminded that Aoba had more than him.

Occasionally, he beat up his brother to show him who was boss, and the younger boy never resisted very hard.

But one night, after he felt he might have gone *too* far, a fire broke out in Ran's room. It started up while he was hanging out with friends, and when he came back home, his father broke his nose for it.

It was supposedly caused by a smoldering cigarette.

Fortunately, it didn't turn into anything worse than a scare—but he didn't remember smoking before he left for the night.

"I'm really glad you didn't get hurt," Aoba said happily, still in elementary school at the time.

Izumii was so overwhelmed by that *smile*, he wasn't able to question his brother about what happened.

After that, he distanced himself from his little brother, and after their parents divorced, they moved to separate places. He heard that his brother filed to have his last name changed to their mother's maiden name, but Ran didn't really care.

All he cared about was staying away from his obnoxious, irritating brother.

Ran was a well-known street thug in the neighborhood; if the situation was going to creep him out that much, he figured he was best off avoiding it.

But now, that brother was coming to him with a serious discussion, saying, "I want some advice."

Up on the rooftop, Izumii was scornful of his younger brother but also slightly apprehensive.

He was a fairly practiced fighter. He hadn't hit Aoba in years, but if this scrawny kid here tried to attack, he knew he could wipe the floor with him. With that reassurance in mind, Izumii grew more confident, relaxed.

Aoba smiled and said, "Actually, I want to ask you a favor."

"What? I got no money to lend you."

"No, it's not that… See, you're famous at schools around the area, right?"

"Huh? The hell you talkin' about?" the older brother asked.

The younger explained, "Well, I made a silly little gang with some friends of mine…"

"A gang? Like what? A little study group?"

"At first, it wasn't meant to be much more than that... But then weirder people started making their way into the group... Older ones. Even some adults, by this point."

Ran was getting irritated that his brother was not getting to the point. But what Aoba said next changed his expression immediately.

"Do you know a Horada and Higa from No. 3 Public Middle School?"

"Wha...?"

He knew those names. They were famous troublemakers in his social circles. Horada had been kicked out of high school, he'd heard, so he never expected to hear the name come from his goody-two-shoes brother's mouth.

"I've never actually met them myself...but they're members of the gang, too."

"...Huh?"

Perhaps he should have laughed it off as a stupid joke. But he couldn't. It made no sense for Aoba to bring up Horada if he wanted it to be funny.

"Things are getting out of hand... I'm worried that if Horada and these adults find out that I'm actually the central figure of the gang, they might do something to mess with me... I'm scared."

He's lying, Ran decided immediately.

Aoba was lying. They were distant, but they were still brothers. He could tell things like that. But he wasn't able to criticize his brother for it.

The story about the gang wasn't a lie.

The story about Horada's kind wasn't a lie.

It was the part about things being "out of hand" that Aoba was lying about.

So Ran lied, too. He boasted to his brother. He uttered empty words meant to convince himself of his own strength on parched breath.

"Man, you're pathetic. So...what do you want me to do? Huh?"

"I'm too scared to run the gang anymore. I don't care about it...so I want *you* to be the leader of my gang now."

"..."

It felt like he might end up being used. But there was no turning back now. If he backed down, he would never again stand above his brother in the pecking order.

With this realization swirling inside of him, he decided that he had to find a way to use his brother instead.

"...Does this gang have a name?"

Aoba flashed an innocent smile and happily, so happily answered.

"Yeah, the name came from my friend."

"We're called the Blue Squares."

♂♀

A year later

Even as they battled with another gang called the Yellow Scarves, Aoba was quiet.

Likewise, his closest companions stayed put, and out of the pride of being the older brother, Ran never asked Aoba for help.

Even when he learned that the police arrested his brother, Aoba said nothing.

And when the Blue Squares fought with the Awakusu-kai and Shizuo Heiwajima, pushing their continued existence to the brink of peril, the young teen merely looked on coldly and said one word.

"...Useless."

♂♀

Several years later, late April, Saitama

"You sure you want this to be the Dollars, Aoba?" asked a boy with a spray can standing in front of a burning motorcycle.

"Yeah. Do it quick before anyone comes," Aoba said. He wore a distant, cold look that he never showed people like Mikado.

They were in a parking garage, late at night. There were no businesses open at this hour and no people passing by at all.

The boy's appearance did not fit the scene surrounding him. There were several motorcycles on fire; their owners sprawled unconscious on the asphalt.

On a nearby wall illuminated by the light of the fires, there was a logo of a sexy woman riding on a tiger that read TORAMARU. The piece would have been an excellent work of art if painted on a proper canvas, but the boy with the can was mercilessly spraying over it with black paint.

Aoba glanced at his work and then spoke to the crowd of youths around him.

"I have no intention of playing up the Blue Squares' name."

"After you gave 'em to your big brother and turned him loose?" a companion jeered.

Aoba smirked. "The name Blue Squares came from a guy named Yatsufusa, anyway."

"Oh yeah, what was that supposed to mean, anyway?" "Hee-hee!"

"Yatsufusa said that we were like a bunch of sharks stranded in the shallows. Each of us was like a little shark stuck in a tiny blue square of territory, desperately protecting it from the others. That's where the name came from," Aoba said. Some of his companions nodded, others looked around in confusion, and some just laughed.

"What does that mean…?" "Hit the books!"

"Are you sure he wasn't actually making fun of us, Aoba?"

"Hee-hee!" "Stupid Yacchi." "Yeah, that is clearly an insult."

"You might be right. But I kind of like it," Aoba said, his smile warm amid the cold laughter of his friends—but lit by the fires of burning motorcycles, that only made him look creepy.

One of the boys, who were entirely unaffected by the sight, looked around and said, "Speaking of which, where did our name provider go?"

"Yatsufusa's out sick. Like always, remember?"

"Yeah, he's got terrible health."

"Hang on! Mitsukuri's tag is spelled 'Dalars' instead."

"Someone stop him." "Aw, who cares." "Hee-hee!"

"So what do we do about the Dollars, anyway, Aoba?"

Aoba answered the raucous crowd. "The biggest sharks get stuck in the shallows and can't swim out. They drown."

From the perspective of his companions, he turned into a shadow against the backdrop of flame. But even without seeing his face, they all knew that he wore a true, giddy smile.

"In order to fully enjoy our youth, we need the great open sea that is the Dollars."

"And why go all the way to Saitama to pick a fight?"

"...The Dollars are wide but shallow. The distance they span might be impressive..."

"But the deeper the water, the easier it is for a shark to swim. Isn't that right?"

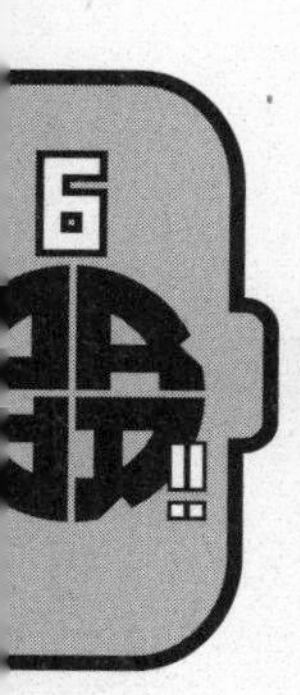

DRRR!! 5
NA9-30
Ryohgo Narita
Intermediate Chapter

May 4, morning, apartment in Shinjuku

"..."

Shizuo Heiwajima stood in front of a door, clenching a fist in irritation.

Blood dripped from between his fingers. The pressure being squeezed into them was unimaginable.

"Son of a...! What a waste of my time!" he fumed, veins popping out on his forehead. If anyone had heard him, they would surely come to the conclusion that his lungs were connected directly to hell, such was the volcanic fury of his tirade.

It was directed at a piece of paper taped to the door.

WE'VE MOVED OFFICES! OUR NEW ADDRESS IS...

The place where Izaya's home/office had been was now completely empty.

The sign would not still be up if a new tenant had moved into the place already. Shizuo was possessed with the urge to kick down the door and destroy everything inside, but the realization that this would only hurt the owner of the property was just barely enough to stifle the rage in his throat.

"...He's wasted my time twice...so I'll murder him twice..."

Shizuo stomped away from the apartment, veins still bulging at the thought of his old nemesis's face.

Only dozens of seconds later, just as Shizuo was leaving the apartment building, a woman pulled the sheet of paper off the door.

"If a trick that crude actually worked on him, this Shizuo must be extremely dense."

Namie Yagiri looked down over the railing of the apartment hallway. She caught sight of the man in the bartender outfit stalking away in a huff and muttered, "This is quite an elaborate ruse, all to push one man into a corner."

She continued watching Shizuo go without much interest and then offered a ghastly suggestion.

"If you can't kill him with a knife, just use poison."

♂♀

As for why Shizuo Heiwajima was heading for Izaya's apartment, that will require rewinding to the morning of the fourth.

"Oh! She's awake!" rang out a voice in Shinra's apartment at six in the morning.

The voice belonged not to Shinra or Tom or Shizuo—but a teenage girl wearing glasses.

Both Shizuo and Tom witnessed Celty asking Shinra to "let her spend the night, since she was attacked by a stranger." Shinra reassured Anri that she didn't need to help out or do anything, but unable to resist, she decided to take over the duty of watching the bedridden little girl.

Shinra got up from his desk and answered, "Okay, I'll be right there." He washed his hands at the sink, picked up a sterilized examination mirror, and headed toward the bedroom.

"Speaking of which, I forgot to tell Celty about the girl."

Well, she seemed really preoccupied. I guess I can tell her later, the doctor thought blearily as he trudged to the room in the back where the girl was sleeping. When he opened the door, he did not see what he was expecting to see.

The little girl was not in her bed anymore, but in the corner of the room, trembling incessantly. And the trembling was not because of the fever.

Her eyes were staring at Shizuo, who was already in the room. He was standing with his arms folded, looking down at her in consternation. "Should I just stay quiet, then?"

"I feel like you talking is just going to agitate her, Shizuo. So, yes, hush up," Shinra advised and held out a hand toward the girl. "How are you feeling? Your complexion looks better, but we should check your temperature first."

But the girl kept her gaze locked onto Shizuo, her eyes pleading angrily.

"Are you going to kill me, *too*?"

"...What do you mean, 'too'?" Shizuo shot back, frowning.

Shinra shook his head sadly. "I knew it. You must have slain one of this poor girl's loved ones..."

"Want me to make you Victim Number One in my personal homicide record?" Shizuo threatened, veins beginning to pulse.

Tom stepped in to calm him down by saying, "Not in front of the kid! You can do it later."

Shinra put a hand to the wary girl's forehead and soothingly noted that her fever was going down. He had a thermometer as well for a proper reading, but the point of the gesture was to calm her down.

Anyone who knew the normal Shinra would have to assume this was a different person entirely. If Celty were there, she would scream, "You've never shown me such a normal smile like this... Aaaah! You lolicon!" and run away from home. That was how reassuring and heartfelt the smile was.

"...Who are you? One of Shizuo Heiwajima's friends?" the girl asked.

"No, I just can't seem to get rid of him. Don't worry. I won't let him hurt you. But to do that, I need you to explain some things first," Shinra said, like a helpful neighborhood physician.

Shizuo felt goose bumps on his back. But if anyone here was going to get the girl to talk, it would be Shinra. So he kept his distance from the girl, listened closely, and tried not to let the creepiness affect him.

Shinra crouched down until he was at eye level with the girl and spoke to her as if she were his own child. "Would you mind telling me your name?"

"...Akane."

"What's your last name, Akane?"

"..."

The moment he asked, the girl named Akane fell silent. He decided that she didn't want to tell him that, so he moved on.

"Does anything hurt? Sore throat, tummy ache, anything like that?"

She shook her head no.

"I see... That's good. Can I ask you about what happened yesterday?"

The girl thought it over for a bit but didn't nod or shake her head. She glanced timidly at Shizuo, and when he met her look through his sunglasses, she twitched in fear.

"Don't worry. He won't do anything. He might be a violent cretin, but he's good at heart. If he was really trying to pick on you, he would have beaten you up already, wouldn't he?"

"..."

"Or did he do something else to you? And that's why you were trying to get him?"

"...No," she squeaked, shaking her head.

Perplexed, Shinra decided to be direct. "Then, why did you want this man in the sunglasses to disappear?"

"..."

She said nothing at first, but after seeing Shinra's disarming smile, she finally admitted, "Because...he's a killer."

"Huh?"

"I heard that a hired killer named Shizuo was going to kill my dad and grandpa. But I can't go back home to them, either, so I didn't know what else to do..."

He had a bad feeling.

Even before he could ask her why she couldn't go back home, a nasty shiver raced through Shinra's body.

The man in the bartender outfit behind him must have felt the same premonition. Shinra heard something that sounded like creaking bone from Shizuo's direction. He forced himself not to look.

"And...what about the stun gun?"

"Someone gave it to me and said it would work on him."

"Who did?"

"Someone who taught me all kinds of things when I ran away from home."

The foreboding intensified. Shinra was beginning to envision a particular face in his mind's eye.

"So this person gave you the stun gun and told you Shizuo was a hit man?"

She nodded.

Shinra tensed up and finally asked, "And…what was his name?"

She hesitated to deliver the finishing blow at first, but over the course of their short conversation, she had decided she trusted Shinra now.

"…Big Brother Izaya."

A chill ran down his back.

He felt a momentary illusion that a demonic god sent to destroy the world was materializing right behind him—and turned slowly, a cold sweat forming, to look at the other man in the room.

There was Shizuo. Smiling kindly.

Huh?! The unfamiliar expression initially plunged Shinra into sheer terror. *Sorry, Celty. I think I might die today*, he thought to himself.

Shizuo said kindly, "Ha-ha, you've got the wrong idea, Akane."

"Oh…?"

"Izaya just has the wrong idea about me. I'm not actually a killer."

"…Really?"

"It's true! Izaya and I are friends—we just had a little fight," Shizuo claimed, shrugging and turning away from Shinra and the girl. "I'm just going to go patch things up with him."

He gave Akane a cheeky wink and left the room, whistling innocently.

When Shinra realized that there was a cold sweat forming all over his body, he thought to himself, so that Akane wouldn't be disturbed, *I wonder if Izaya is tired of life or something…*

Tom walked out the front door and closed it behind him, then called out to Shizuo ahead.

"Way to hold it in. You deserve the People's Honor Award or something."

"...Thank you, Tom," Shizuo grunted to his boss without looking back. "I have a request."

"What's that?"

"If I kill someone and get arrested today, please ask the boss to say that I was fired as of yesterday."

"..."

Tom had plenty of thoughts to share, but he kept them to himself as he watched Shizuo head down the stairs.

He stood in the walkway of the apartment building, watching the scenery below, and then pulled out a cigarette and lit it. He took a deep drag and exhaled a comment to himself with the smoke.

"Better call the boss and tell him Shizuo took the day off..."

♂♀

May 4, late morning, art gallery, Ikebukuro

It was a pristine interior, full of painting frames hanging on exquisite wallpaper.

But the voice that spoke within it had very little in common with fine art.

"...Just think about it. For the price of just a single cup of coffee a day, this work of art, a source of pure joy, can be yours. It's just the first step to being a winner in life," the woman said with a plastic smile.

The young man, his face bandaged, looked lovestruck. "Hmm, it's very tempting. But if I spent all that money at once, I don't know what my girlfriend would think."

"I believe she will be utterly impressed when she sees this painting on the wall of your residence. Coming across the right piece of art is as fateful as locking eyes with the girl of your dreams. It's extremely rare to come across a piece by the great Karnard Strasburg, even if it is a print!"

She was in the midst of a sales pitch over a particular piece that had been placed next to the table. The young man she was trying to sell it to had been there for over an hour. But he was staring directly at the saleswoman's face, not showing the least amount of interest in the painting itself.

"Personally, I find *you* to be much more interesting than the painting."

"Well, if you want to know, I find myself very attracted to men who would buy paintings like this."

"Really?"

"Really! I mean, people who can spend money on their dreams are just irresistible!"

The art was indeed from a famed master—but it was silk-screened on a poster, no more than a cheap mass-market item. She kept calling it a "print," claiming that it was a rare item with a serial number.

In fact, it could be bought for less than thirty thousand yen, but the price she quoted to him was 1.28 million.

If you wanted a rare Karnard Strasburg piece for that price, you could get one that was a lithograph rather than silk-screened—but the saleswoman continued to insist that the cheap print was, in fact, a valuable work of art.

He's gotta give in soon.

The chief of the sales team, watching from a distance, was certain that the customer would buy the painting. If he still held back, the chief could try the "you wasted our time and business, so just sign the check" method. This was the kind of place that would get down and dirty, if needed.

But the bandaged man's reaction was too abnormal for such orthodox means to work.

The bandaged young man spotted the sales chief and beckoned him over, beaming. He approached the table, assuming that the deal was as good as closed.

"Is something the matter, sir?"

"Well, actually, I don't have any money. And this babe here says she really needs me to buy it. So I've decided to work out a deal."

"Yes, sir, thank you very much!" the chief grinned, assuming they were going to work out a finance plan. The young man with the eyepatch grinned back.

"Put 'er there."

"Pardon?"

To the chief's confusion, the man covered in gauze held out the palm of his hand as if to receive something. But the contract and pen were already sitting on the table. What else could he want?

He was just wondering if the customer was expecting a business card when he shockingly heard, "One million two hundred and eighty yen, she says. You can give me your card, if you don't have the cash."

"…Huh?"

The sales chief had no idea what the young man meant.

He continued, "Well, I mean, the lady says she needs this. But I don't have the money. A man can't cause trouble for a lady, now, can he? But you seem like you've got the means. You're probably the owner of this gallery or something, right? If you can buy all this expensive art to hang in here, you've gotta be loaded."

"Umm…"

"Money should be spent on women. You're a man, so you should buy this painting to help her out. Give me the one million two hundred and eighty and I can handle the rest."

"Sir, you must be joking," the chief mumbled, his face tense. The next moment, it froze entirely.

"…What? …Joking?"

Abruptly, the eyepatch-covered face turned sharp, cold, and undeniably cruel. The shift from when he was talking to the woman was so sudden and startling that the sales chief instantly realized, *This guy isn't a regular patron.*

"When did I tell a joke? When did I make you laugh? Huh?" he said, getting to his feet and approaching the chief's nose.

The saleswoman finally recognized what was happening, and her face went pale. She said, "Um, s-sir?"

The young man spun around on the spot and flashed her a smile and thumbs-up. "Don't worry, miss. He's gonna buy it. Like you said, not only will it make his life better, he'll have the women screaming over him. Any man with money would buy it!"

The sales chief shot the woman a look that said, *Why did you bring him in here?*

She looked back at him with teary eyes that pleaded, *I didn't pitch him anything; he just started hitting on me on the street and followed me in here*, but that was a little too detailed for mere eyes to get across.

But there was another person who saw her about to cry: the unbelievable customer.

"Hey, guy."

"Y-yes?!"

"You just shot her a dirty look, didn't you?" he accused, full of righteous fury.

The chief was taken aback—which was ironic because it was usually his job to threaten customers. "H...huh...?"

"I don't know if you're her boss or whatever, but she's been tryin' her best to walk me through this whole practice, since I'm new to it. Who the hell do you think you are, staring her down?"

"Wha...? Um, sir, this is a private company matter. It has nothing to do with you..."

"So if it's none of my business, that means I'm free to hit you?" he threatened, cracking his neck as he took a step forward.

"S-sir, I'll call the poli—" the chief started to say, and then the possibility arose in his head that he might die before the police arrived. He had plenty of experience with odd guests, but the attitude coming from this person was something he'd never seen on this level before.

And right as the menacing youth crouched down to do *something*—a ringtone went off in his shirt pocket.

"..."

The young man stopped, picked up his phone, and held it to his ear.

"It's me... Ah, gotcha. Where are you now? Huh? ...The hell? That's right outside this building. Actually, all of you come inside here right now. There's an asshole here who doesn't know how a lady feels... Oh yeah? Tsk... Fine, fine. I'm coming out."

The man in the eyepatch and bandages hung up and glared at the sales chief.

"I'm gonna come back here later to make damn sure you bought this lady her painting..."

♂♀

Outside of art gallery, Ikebukuro

"So you found this Dollars guy?" Chikage Rokujou asked of his fellow Toramaru gang member as he exited the gallery.

The man in the leather jacket grunted confirmation and reported, "He's a half-Japanese guy named Walker Yumasaki, and he's supposedly pretty well known within the Dollars."

"Weird name. Where is he now?"

"Well...," the man in the jacket mumbled. He jutted his chin up a bit to signal the gallery building in front of them.

"He followed a woman into that building right before you walked out of it."

♂♀

Inside the gallery

I thought I was going to die...

The sales chief was relieved that the man finally left. Then, he heard a different visitor's voice. It was not the usual business talk—it sounded as though there was trouble after all.

What is it now? he wondered.

A young man was arguing passionately in front of a painting by an illustrator who went by the name Suzy Yasuda.

"I mean, this is just silk-screened, so even with the frame, at this size the base cost would be twenty-four thousand yen, right? I have great respect for this illustrator, so I'd be willing to pay a million yen for this masterpiece! However, I cannot make this deal unless I have a guarantee that at least eight hundred thousand of that will go to the artist."

"Er, well..."

"Besides, this piece was not originally drawn to be silk-screened. And selling it with a serial number as if it was supposed to be printed is just tarnishing the true value of the work. Did Suzy really allow you to print and sell this? This? I mean, there are way too many holes in your story! It doesn't get a single fraction of Suzy's appeal across to the buyer! It completely ruins her mystique! Where did you get these level-zero powers, anyway?! Listen, the root of Suzy's illustrations goes back to..."

"Ch-chief!" pleaded the sales clerk.

The chief raced over and recognized the narrow-eyed half-Western boy. He put his head in his hands. "Not you again, sir! Please leave at once!"

Once the chief harangued the young man out of the building, he turned to scold the woman who had been soliciting customers on the street.

"You're new here, but let me warn you: That half-Japanese customer is not to be trifled with! Even if he happens to look like a very easy mark!"

"Y-yes, sir."

The stressed-out chief, a master at underhanded sales strategies, muttered to himself, "I think I need to get out of this business..."

"That guy dressed as a bartender smashes the place up right as I start working here... The Awakusu-kai stroll right in and demand the originals we copy... It's just insane, really..."

♂♀

Right around the time the sales chief felt like he was going to get an ulcer, Chikage Rokujou started following Yumasaki as he exited the gallery.

"...That's him? Doesn't look the part."

"Well, that's just what the Dollars are like. You can't identify 'em in a crowd like that. A couple of our guys who raided Ikebukuro last month got beat by his friend, some asshole named Kadota. From what I hear, Kadota's got a lot of pull within the Dollars."

"Ahhh...," Chikage muttered, following his prey by sight. Up ahead, a woman dressed in black stopped Yumasaki. Next to her was a fierce-looking man with a knit cap who was speaking with Yumasaki on obviously friendly terms.

"Ah, that's him! Kadota is the guy in the beanie."

"...They've got a girl. No action this time, then. We'll just watch."

"Got it."

The Dollars trio wandered around Sunshine Street for a while longer, and as they reached the Tokyu Hands building, Kadota said something to Yumasaki and the woman and then walked off on his own.

The pair crossed at the light to go toward Sunshine City, while Kadota continued south along the Metropolitan Expressway.

"I'll take it from here. You meet up with the rest."

"But—"

"Just go."

"Got it."

With his companion out of the way, Chikage continued following Kadota. But after a while, his gaze stopped on a building nearby.

He stopped walking momentarily, forgetting even that he was busy trailing a target.

"...Right in the middle of Ikebukuro...there's an all-girls' school...?!"

The leader of Toramaru was rooted to the spot for most of a minute, standing at the entrance of a girls' academy located right near Raira Academy. Because of the vacation, there did not happen to be any girls in the vicinity right now.

But I gotta hold out hope... No! I got more important things to do now.

He came back to his senses and shook his head. Suddenly, he heard someone speak in a cold voice behind him.

"...You want something with us?"

"..."

Chikage spun around and saw the man with the beanie, the one he was supposed to be trailing. "Oh. You knew I was following you."

"Yeah. But I began to doubt my own instincts when you stopped in front of the all-girls' school," Kadota said, cracking his neck. He asked Chikage, "So who are you? I don't think I've ever met you before, but at least I know you're not the kind of scum who'd target a guy escorting a lady."

"My name's Chikage Rokujou... I think I'd get along with you," he grinned, and then he shook his head sadly. "But...you're with the Dollars, right?"

"...Yeah, you might say that."

"It's a shame. I heard a rumor that Shizuo Heiwajima's also in the Dollars. Is that for real?" he asked.

"...I think that's the case, but I don't believe he thinks of himself as being a member of anything," Kadota replied honestly.

"Yeah, he's one of *those* guys, huh? I see... So you're not all on the same page together."

"?"

"...But still, that's got nothin' to do with us."

Right at that moment, Kadota's cell phone rang, as if on cue.

"Go on, get it. I'll wait."

"It's an e-mail," Kadota said, looking at the screen without letting down his guard. The ringtone had to be for messages relating to the Dollars. He opened it up promptly, wondering if it had something to do with the man right in front of him.

"..."

Kadota squinted at the contents of the message, and then he turned up to glare at Chikage.

"What's up?"

"...Hey, punk."

The message on his phone was an emergency alert—that Dollars were being *attacked all over Ikebukuro.*

"Why did you— No, why did all of you people come here?" Kadota demanded, staring down the other man in worry and anger.

Chikage, meanwhile, stared right back into Kadota's eyes. He shrugged. "We just came to pay for the fight we were sold."

"Keep the change. I don't need it."

♂♀

At that moment, inside the abandoned factory

As Mikado tried to extract the term *Blue Squares* from the recesses of his mind to put a meaning to Aoba's shocking revelation, his cell phone suddenly erupted with the arrival of an e-mail.

Similar notifications and vibrations went off on the phones of the other boys around them, all at once.

—!

The notification was the sound Mikado used for Dollars-related messages—which led him to a major realization.

I should have figured… They're all Dollars, too.

A group all gathered in one place. Ringtones going off all at once.

The scale was much, much smaller, but it reminded Mikado of a scene he experienced a year earlier. The realization shook him.

And even worse than that was the content of the e-mail: that members of the Dollars were under attack.

"I think it's started," Aoba said as he checked the same message on his phone, his smile never wavering.

"Started…? What's started…?"

"Toramaru's revenge… The guys from Saitama," Aoba replied. Mikado felt his vision warp.

Is this…real life?

Was this boy really the same kid from school who grinned innocently at everything? Well, he certainly had that same smile right now.

But Mikado couldn't connect the things that Aoba was saying with reality as he knew it.

"Why…would you attack people in Saitama? Why are you doing this…?"

"It was thanks to them that our little Ikebukuro tour got torn to shreds. So this was a little payback… Does that work for you?"

"…"

Mikado swallowed. He had no words.

Based on what he heard so far, he had to assume that he wasn't going to elicit Aoba's true intentions here. Clutching his phone, Mikado decided to attempt a dialogue with the younger boy.

"The Blue Squares… I've heard of them. I think…they were a color gang around here years ago… And after a war with the Yellow Scarves, a number of them were claimed by the other gang…from what I hear."

A number of the boys in the factory whistled in admiration. Even Aoba's eyes were sparkling in surprise.

"You know a lot more than I imagined. I'm impressed!"

"Why would you tell me…tell me these things?"

"Because I trust you. Is that such a bad thing?"

"It's not an answer... What do you want from me?" Mikado demanded, his confusion only deepening.

"That's a good question. I was hoping to do this after you knew a little bit more about us...but I guess I could just start off by asking you first."

Aoba looked up at Mikado, still sitting on the pile of metal beams, his eyes sparkling.

"Leader," he prompted.

"Huh...?"

"I'm not asking you to be the leader of the Dollars. That would conflict with the ethos of the Dollars, I suppose."

Giggling.

Mocking.

For some reason, the other boys present all broke into laughter, the sound undulating rhythmically off the walls of the empty factory. And riding atop that rhythm like poetry, Aoba's words melted into the air of the room, rattling Mikado with their implication.

"...Instead, we want you to be the leader of the *Blue Squares.*"

"Uh..."

"We'll just hang back and follow you."

He couldn't keep up. It was too sudden, too illogical.

It felt like someone was asking him to become an Arab oil monarch tomorrow. If Yumasaki and Karisawa had mentioned it, he would have assumed they were making a manga reference. That was how baffling the request was to Mikado.

"Why...why would I—?"

"Well, there are a number of reasons, but mostly it's because you occupy a special position in the Dollars."

"Special position...?" Mikado repeated robotically.

Aoba helpfully explained, "To be brief, it's because *you are the founder of the Dollars.*"

"...!"

"Is that a surprise? We have our own information network, you know."

Aoba was neither intimidated by nor was he patronizing to the stunned Dollars' founder. He simply put his intentions into words that spoke for themselves.

"You can use us any way you want. If you decide you want to end this war, and command us to go and grovel at Toramaru's feet so they

can beat us to a pulp…then we'll have no choice but to obey. We'll take it. But if we survive and make it out of the hospital, then you really will be our leader… On the other hand, if you command us to crush Toramaru and stop them from harming our fellow Dollars, we'll use whatever means necessary."

"You know…I can't do…*either!* It's out of the question!" Mikado said, finding his authority at last. He shook his head vigorously. "What makes you think I would accept such a thing…? If you want to avoid gang warfare, just pretend you're not in the Dollars and stay out of it. That's the type of person I am. I'm not meant to stand on your shoulders!"

It was a true cry from the heart. That was how he meant it and how it felt coming out.

But Aoba only got to his feet and leaned in close.

In a tiny voice that only Mikado could hear, he muttered, "That's not true."

He looked delighted, so delighted.

"After all…"

"Huh…?"

"At this very moment…

…you're *smiling*, aren't you?"

♂♀

At that moment, within the factory grounds

It was a negotiation taking place in total privacy.

No matter what choice Mikado made, only those involved in the matter would know.

Except that a third party was, in fact, listening in at that very moment.

And depending on how loosely you wanted to define it, they were very much involved.

Ummm…

Celty Sturluson was on the outside of the abandoned factory, hiding in the shadows around a window.

...What's going on here?

Her sense of hearing could pick up the conversation inside with ease. It sounded like the uniquely aggressive bravado of young delinquents, but the boy at the center of it was someone she knew.

Am I actually witnessing a major turning point in Mikado's life?

The irony was that it wasn't even the group of boys that had brought her here.

Celty only spent a few minutes back at Shinra's apartment the previous night. She was surprised to learn that Shizuo and his workmate had been there, but there was more important business to cover: She explained the situation with Anri and asked Shinra to let the girl stay the night, then left again.

The reason she left was simple: She had to search for the girl in the photo, the granddaughter of the Awakusu boss.

According to Shiki, the girl was bouncing between twenty-four-hour manga cafés and family restaurants. It seemed unlikely that such a girl could stay at a late-night restaurant by herself without being reported to the police, but she clearly had some special trick to living out of a restaurant.

But how would she shower? When Celty peered into an actual manga café (with funny looks and warnings about wearing her helmet indoors), she was surprised to learn that the cafés were putting in showers now.

In addition to this, she was rotating around the homes of friends from school and acquaintances from the Internet, which made it difficult for the yakuza's information network to pick up details.

Shiki claimed that they would inform her once they found the girl, but the thought of those dangerous, armed men on the move made Celty afraid for this unfamiliar girl and pressed her into action.

All night long, she prowled around Ikebukuro—without realizing that the girl had been inside her apartment all along.

Celty wound up cycling through restaurants until morning but never found the girl—and when she returned to digging into the identity of the mystery attackers from earlier, the trail of black thread led her to the abandoned factory.

Wow...my shadow really will stretch for miles and miles, she noted with surprised admiration when she saw that the thread was still intact. When the slender line of shadow touched the ground, it rejoined her real shadow, where it would not tangle on anything or anyone.

Celty could manipulate the shadow at will, making it act like a liquid or even a gas if she wanted. If she ran it around a single building hundreds of times, she could still retrieve all of it within mere seconds.

I feel like that cat-shaped robot that came from the future with all its helpful tools. But I can return to that later, she thought and focused on the situation before her. *What is it with me and this run-down old factory?*

She was interested in what choice Mikado would make, but was it right of her to listen in? A wave of terrible guilt washed over her, but Celty couldn't force herself to move or stop eavesdropping.

And she, too, was being observed by someone else.

♂♀

At that moment, inside Russia Sushi

"So what is it?"

"There are signs the two of them have been around Ikebukuro. I thought I ought to tell you."

They were speaking Russian—the familiar visitor Egor, as well as the brusque owner of the sushi shop, who asked, "You said the other day that these are people we don't know?"

"Yes."

"Well, it's true that I don't know this Slon fellow, but Vorona is Drakon's little daughter, isn't she?"

"When I said you don't know them, I was being truthful. She's not the girl you once knew, Denis."

Simon was out luring in customers for the approaching lunch hour, when the restaurant would open, so the only ones in the building were Egor and Denis, the owner.

"It's still her, no matter how much she changes. That's what Colonel Lingerin would say," Denis noted with disinterest.

"Well, er…if you look at things the same way that Lingerin does, yes," Egor sighed. "Did you happen to hear anything last night?"

"…I heard what sounded like one distant shot from an anti-matériel rifle."

"I heard it, too. That was probably Vorona and Slon. And it didn't just 'sound like' that, it was the very anti-matériel rifle that they took from the company."

"…"

The sushi chef silently polished his knife as Egor rubbed the bandages wrapped around his face. He came to a serious conclusion.

"It will do no one any favors if we don't stop her soon. For her sake, for Drakon's sake, and for Tokyo's sake. And of course…for your sake, since you love this place so much."

♂♀

At that moment, rooftop, building next to abandoned factory

"Unused factory building. The information was in error. Location is gathering place of delinquent youth."

"It looks like the Black Rider is hiding from the children… Should we snipe from here?" Slon asked as he peered through the scope.

Vorona shook her head. "Rider survived after yesterday's shot—true monster. Failed attempt will only reveal our location. Fatal mistake."

Vorona and Slon were on standby on the roof of a building within a reasonable distance from the factory. They were set up so they could see the majority of the factory grounds and watched Celty as she followed the black thread in.

If they only wanted to find her, they just had to follow the thread the other direction. But they were enemies, of course, and it would be foolish to head straight into a face-to-face confrontation.

Instead, they left Vorona's motorcycle inside the empty factory to lure the Black Rider there—and just moments after that, the strange group of boys appeared. Now the rider was crouched in the shadows outside of the window, hiding from them.

But of course, she was openly visible to Vorona and Slon. The

Russian woman continued watching for a while, sucked in a deep breath, and muttered, "We will follow the monster. Target child might be found at the end of this."

Slon sighed and commented, "You're enjoying yourself, Vorona."

"Affirmation. It has become more enjoyable."

Vorona's flat expression, that was a gift from her father, twisted slightly with her warped words of love.

"I like Ikebukuro. Half disappointment, half envy. A bit of hope. That is love."

"I have decided to love Ikebukuro. Affirmation."

♂♀

At that moment, office building, Ikebukuro

"That son of a… I told him never to come back to Ikebukuro…"

In an office building far from the shopping center of the neighborhood, Shizuo was furiously climbing the stairs.

"Now he thinks he can just open up an office here…"

He reached the third floor and set his sights on a door straight ahead. The address on the sheet of paper pasted on his old office was correct. There was no sign on the door or wall, but there weren't any other tenants in the building, either.

Guess I'll pretend to be a customer to get him to open up.

He knocked on the office door.

"…"

There was no response.

He spotted a doorbell to the side and tried ringing that—still no response.

Next, he attempted to listen through the door to see if it was vacant inside, but he heard the sounds of a TV or radio coming from within.

So he thinks he can pretend not to be home? Shizuo fumed and grabbed the knob so he could force the door open…

Huh?

The door wasn't locked. It opened without any resistance.

What the hell? He didn't even lock up.

Shizuo let go of the knob, which was now molded into the shape of his palm, and strode into the office, not bothering to hide his irritation.

The office was split into a number of smaller rooms, and the first one had bookshelves along the wall, packed with countless files and materials.

...Is this what an info dealer's office looks like? Shizuo wondered suspiciously. He continued toward the back in search of his archenemy.

What he saw there was...

"..."

"........"

"..............Huh?"

Seconds passed after he first saw it.

Shizuo could not initially process the sight before him.

It was actually quite a simple scene, one that an objective observer could instantly identify.

But for the subjective viewer in this case, it was almost impossible to piece together.

He was looking at three blobs of flesh, dressed in suits.

One in front of the TV, which was still on.

One slumped in a chair.

One driven into the thin wall that separated room from room.

It took some time for Shizuo to realize that they were all "done in," as it were.

The face of the man in front of the TV was half-pulverized.

The head of the man sitting in the chair had been twisted 180 degrees.

The spine of the man driven into the wall was broken at an odd angle from the rest of his torso.

There was one initial thing that unified all of them, as far as he could tell.

All three had been dispatched using what appeared to be bare-handed means.

"…"

It had been a long time since he saw a dead body.

Shizuo had never committed murder, but through his various exploits over the years starting from high school, he had seen corpses on a number of occasions.

If he hadn't, he might have thrown up on the spot, such was the level of carnage on display.

How long had he stood on the spot?

Wait, you gotta be kidding me. Why are there dead bodies in Izaya's office?

Surprise turned to suspicion in Shizuo's mind, and the questions led to more questions.

Hang on… Is this really Izaya's office…?

Just then, someone behind him bellowed, "Hey, you! Who said you could come…in…?"

Shizuo spun around to see a young man with a shaved head. He looked imposing enough on his own, but he stopped in his tracks with obvious uncertainty when he recognized Shizuo.

He looked from Shizuo to the blobs of flesh. His eyes went wide, and his mouth started working like a goldfish's.

"Y-y-you, why, why, why you…why you…"

The man with the shaved head put a hand on the wall behind him and then ran toward the entrance in a panic.

There had been no time to explain anything. Shizuo snorted in confusion and put a hand to his chin to think.

That was when he realized that he had been framed, in the most direct and stunning way possible.

Less than a minute later, the bald-headed man returned with a gun, fearfully looking for Shizuo. But Shizuo was already gone. The only sound in the office was the whistling wind from the open third-story window.

A few seconds more after that, the room echoed with the man's furious voice as he yelled into the phone.

"Shizuo… It was Shizuo Heiwajima! I recognized him! Call Mr. Shiki right away!"

"That little prick just killed three of our boys!"

And as of that moment, Shizuo Heiwajima's peace of mind and his desire to lead a quiet life were utterly eradicated.

♂♀

May 4, midday, underground east exit of Ikebukuro Station, front of the Ikefukuro Owl Café

"Don't worry. The person coming to see us is very nice," Anri reassured Akane, who looked up at her and nodded.

Akane's fever was totally gone, and with Shizuo being gone now, it seemed that the mental stress plaguing her had eased. Shinra gave his stamp of approval as well, and so Anri decided to take the frightened girl outside to buoy her spirits.

She was worried about the possibility the girl might try to run away, but Akane claimed that if she ran across "that Shizuo person," she would try to hear him out properly this time, so Anri took her at her word.

Plus, the mention of Izaya Orihara's name was very concerning for Anri, too. She and Izaya had faced off as enemies once before, although that was less Anri and more Saika at work.

On top of that, there was the sudden attack the previous night, as well as the girl's claim that her father and grandfather were going to be killed.

Shinra suggested that it might be dangerous to go out, but it also seemed very unlikely that any fights would break out among the bustling crowds of Ikebukuro in the middle of the day.

When she explained that she had an arrangement to meet some school friends, Shinra said, "Okay, I'll tell Celty when she gets back. Once she has some free time after work, I'll send her to keep an eye on you. Of course, if Shizuo was around, I'd have *him* be your bodyguard," and allowed them to leave the apartment.

But now that they were actually out, Anri suspected that it might have been careless of her after all. If that assailant from yesterday wasn't the type to hesitate in the middle of the open public, she might be exposing innocent Akane to danger.

So Anri waited, tense and wary.

She wanted Mikado and Aoba to arrive as quickly as possible to bring the sense of normalcy and security that they provided her.

But she simply didn't realize that the normalcy of Ikebukuro, particularly around the people she knew, had already been shattered.

And thus Anri Sonohara did not yet realize that they were taking a step into that broken city.

♂♀

A dark place, Ikebukuro

Izaya Orihara's cell phone also received the message about the Dollars under attack.

But that wasn't all.

He was getting messages from multiple pet sources of his with similar information. Every once in a while, there were details of an entirely different kind.

Izaya glanced over all of this info equally in the darkness. He mumbled, "Those little Blue Squares brats. I guess they were after the same thing, but only up to a point."

Half-excited and half-irritated, he envisioned a particular boy's face.

"But that's all right. If you think about it, Aoba Kuronuma is another sweet little junior of mine from Raira. I suppose…I accept his challenge."

He fiddled with his phone and spoke aloud—to the darkness or to himself?

"Now I will work directly to outdo you in an honest battle of wits."

Izaya sent a few messages off and then reached for a knob in the midst of the dark.

"As fellow black sheep among the sea that is the Dollars..."

The door opened, filling his eyes with the blinding noon sun. He stared balefully up at it.

"...We ought to get along and cannibalize each other."

Izaya Orihara laughed.

It was unclear just how much he knew about Aoba Kuronuma and his cohorts.

Did he have a plan to crush them, or was he happy to be obliterated in the attempt either way?

Izaya's smile was endlessly human, and that was what made him seem so unnatural.

His laugh was only the starting point.

It was the beginning of an extremely twisted story.

PRESENTED BY

Ryohgo Narita

CAST

Celty Sturluson
Shinra Kishitani

Mikado Ryuugamine
Anri Sonohara
Masaomi Kida

Izaya Orihara
Shizuo Heiwajima

Akane Awakusu
Chikage Rokujou

Aoba Kuronuma
Kururi Orihara
Mairu Orihara

Walker Yumasaki
Erika Karisawa
Kyouhei Kadota

Namie Yagiri
Shiki
Tom Tanaka

Vorona
Slon
Lingerin Douglanikov
Drakon
Denis
Simon Brezhnev

ILLUSTRATIONS & VISUAL CONCEPTS — Suzuhito Yasuda (AWA Studio)

DESIGN — Yoshihiko Kamabe

EDITING — Sue Suzuki
Atsushi Wada

PUBLISHING — ASCII Media Works

DISTRIBUTION — Kadokawa Shoten

AFTERWORD

Hello, I'm Ryohgo Narita. It's nice to see you again.

Well, thanks to all of you, *Durarara!!* has reached a fifth volume.

...But you'll have to pardon me, as it's just the first half of a two-part story. I switched things up this time to have the adult characters getting into the act, but this is still at its heart a story of love centered around Ikebukuro. I think.

As usual, some characters don't get much time to shine, but once I'm finished concluding this tale in Volume 6, I plan to write more of a romantic soap opera based around Namie, Seiji, and Mika. I have no idea if anyone actually wants to read that, but I choose to believe that there are many Namie fans out there.

At any rate! I want to get the next book out to you as soon as possible, but I'm afraid I've really gone and damaged myself with bronchitis this time, so my usual writing carnage will involve lots of rest. On the other hand, all of that carnage is making me get out of shape. I need to get back on that Wii Fit.

So anyway, just as he was exhausted in both body and spirit, a bolt of lightning hit unsuspecting Ryohgo Narita!

It's a manga adaptation!

As of the April 18, 2009, issue of Square Enix's *G Fantasy* magazine, *Durarara!!* will be a manga! A fresh new breath of air will be blown into the world of *Durarara!!* courtesy of the artist Akiyo Satorigi!

As a matter of fact, when I heard about the manga idea, I was secretly wondering, "But...how will they handle the chat scenes...?" Well, that's something I'm looking forward to learning. In fact, these novels are really unsuited to a visual medium! I have nothing but thanks to Mr. Kuma from Square Enix for pushing so hard for this project.

Even I don't know what sort of manga this will turn out to be. As yet another reader like all of you, I can't wait to find out how the world of Ikebukuro comes to life in manga form!

That may have been a huge mental boost for me, but I was still physically exhausted, so I enjoyed a few days of rest and relaxation after turning in the manuscript.

To fully enjoy my mini-vacation, I joined a number of other authors (some of whom might have been on the clock before deadlines, so I will not divulge any names) in an all-night board-game tournament at the home of Mr. Saegusa, a fellow writer. When I first saw his place, with two entire walls covered with board games both domestic and foreign, I nearly screamed. Gamers are scary.

A few days later, I visited the new home of my friend Mr. Sigsawa, where we played *Fallout 3* and *Test Drive*, then watched through all of *Astro Fighter Sunred* and the latest episode of *Toradora!* Mr. Sigsawa is a devout practitioner of safe driving in the real world, so watching him barrel all over Hawaii in *Test Drive* on a TV screen the size of a wall was really fun for the whole group.

...Wait... I didn't really get much rest at all, did I?

Anyway, my break is over, which means it's back to the carnage again.

I currently have a little story I wrote for April Fools' last year running as a special bonus add-on to a magazine called *TYPE-MOON Ace*, Volume 2 (Thanks, everyone at TYPE-MOON!), as well as a number of other projects in the works, but my Dengeki workload is still at full throttle.

After *Durarara!!* I'll have *Hariyama-san* or *Baccano! 1710* or *Vamp!* or perhaps straight into *Durarara!!* Volume 7. Whatever happens, there will be no time to stop and breathe. No time at all...!

Even as I begin to lose sight of where I end and the work begins, I've been enjoying video games as a means to get back to my basics.

Meanwhile, my artists are becoming visible all over the game industry, what with Yasuda in *Devil Survivor* and Enami in *Star Ocean 4*.

It feels strange, having that world be so distant and yet so close to me. Speaking of which, *Devil Survivor* is seriously way too fun to be allowed. If I get started on that topic, no number of pages will contain me, so I'll hold back. Meanwhile, *Fallout 3* on the Xbox 360 is blowing my mind as well, but the same limitations apply.

*The following is the usual list of acknowledgements.

To my editor, who has to put up with my constant nonsense at all times, Mr. Papio. To managing editor Suzuki, editor Jasmine Tokuda, and the rest of the editorial office, including one Mr. M who served as the model for an Awakusu-kai character.

To the proofreaders, whom I give a hard time by being so late with submissions. To all the designers involved with the production of the book. To all the people at Media Works involved in marketing, publishing, and sales.

To my family who do so much for me in so many ways, my friends, and the people of "S City."

To all the writers and illustrators working with Dengeki Bunko for their inspiration and permission.

To Suzuhito Yasuda, for providing such wonderful illustrations, despite being busy with his work on *Devil Survivor* and his *Yozakura* series.

And to all the readers who checked out this book.

Thank you all so very, very, very much!

January 2009 — "Heading into playthrough number three of Shin Megami Tensei: Devil Survivor*"*

Ryohgo Narita

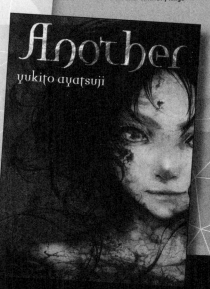